D1147544

THE CROWS ARE CRYING

THE CROWS ARE CRYING

A Novel

Marie Campbell

iUniverse, Inc.

New York Lincoln Shanghai

The Crows are Crying

Copyright © 2007 by Marie Campbell

All rights reserved. No part of this book may be used or reproduced by any means, graphic, electronic, or mechanical, including photocopying, recording, taping or by any information storage retrieval system without the written permission of the publisher except in the case of brief quotations embodied in critical articles and reviews.

iUniverse books may be ordered through booksellers or by contacting:

iUniverse
2021 Pine Lake Road, Suite 100
Lincoln, NE 68512
www.iuniverse.com
1-800-Authors (1-800-288-4677)

Because of the dynamic nature of the Internet, any Web addresses or links contained in this book may have changed since publication and may no longer be valid.

This is a work of fiction. All of the characters, names, incidents, places, organizations, and dialogue in this novel are either the products of the author's imagination or are used fictitiously.

ISBN: 978-0-595-47199-7 (pbk)
ISBN: 978-0-595-91480-7 (ebk)

Printed in the United States of America

CHAPTER 1

───────────▼───────────

He stood looking down the valley—a tall handsome man, with a crop of reddish fair hair, broad shoulders. Looking at him, one got the feeling of strength. About his mouth and eyes there was gentleness. But, there was a devil may care attitude about him as he made his way down the valley.

This was Jack Ryan, newly arrived in Scotland from Tipperary in Ireland, here to work in the coalmine in this valley.

It was going to be hard for him to work under the ground when all his life he had farmed. His thoughts went back to the farm he had left only that morning. He had tried so hard to make it pay, but year after year things got more desperate; then two years in a row the crops had failed and that was the end.

His parents had died within a year of each other; all their hard work and struggle keeping the farm going had taken its toll. In the end he had been forced to sell to pay all the mounting debts.

So here he was looking down at Loadie, a little mining village. Two rows of small cottages lined the dusty road, belonging he guessed, to the mine owners. At the far end was the village shop, the blacksmith's smiddy and the village pub, and a little bit further on all the activity of the coal mine.

The good-natured big Irishman soon settled in at the mine, for he was a good worker. On a Saturday night he was in great demand in the pub, singing his Irish ballads. He was twenty-four years old and stood a lot of teasing because he never bothered with the village girls, who were always, as the saying goes, "Giving him the eye." He had managed to find a good place to stay, with a Mrs Lafferty, a widow, who treated him more like a son than a lodger. It was her suggestion that he should visit Stirling, the nearest town to Loadie.

"You have been here for months," she said to him. "It's time you bought some decent clothes"

She was right, Jack thought to himself. Working six days a week, twelve hours a day, he had no time for getting "dressed" up. When he went to the pub on a Saturday night he wore the same clothes that he had travelled from Ireland in. They were pretty shabby now.

"You can get a lift on Saturday morning on the Dray cart," Mrs Lafferty continued. "But you will have to walk back"

Stirling was about five miles from Loadie, but the people in the village thought nothing of the walk, sometimes coming back heavily laden with all their purchases. When Saturday morning came, Jack was up bright and early and left quite excited. This was the first time he had left the village in nearly a year. All the bits and pieces he had needed he had brought at the village shop. But, Mrs Lafferty was right, he did need some dress clothes.

He wandered about the streets enjoying Stirling after the quiet of Loadie. Passing a draper's shop, he spotted some nice shirts in the window. A little self-consciously, he went in. It seemed as if they sold everything in the shop. There were three departments—one department, all gents clothing, the middle department devoted, it seemed, to ladies wear, and yet another was taken over with all kinds of household things. There was no one serving in the gents department, but quite a lot of noise was coming from the ladies department. A large fat lady was giving the young girl serving her a hard time.

"Do waken up girl!" she was shouting. "I told you last week that I needed the dress by today … did you forget that I ordered it?"

"No madam," the girl replied in a soft voice. "It's just that the traveller was delayed this week. He may be in later today."

Jack felt sorry for the young assistant. He looked at her more closely and his heart gave a quickened beat. "Gosh!" he thought—she was pretty and dainty, not much higher than his shoulder. Dark hair tumbled down her back. Large brown eyes filled with tears as the stout woman screamed on.

Jack felt compelled to go to her rescue. But just then a severe looking elderly woman appeared from the back shop.

"Now … Now," she said, "What's all the noise." She turned to the young girl. "Elizabeth, will you please go and serve the gentleman waiting next door. I will sort things out here."

Elizabeth looked up at the tall Irishman. "Can I help you Sir?" she said in her soft voice.

"Well, yes" Jack stammered, suddenly all tongue-tied. "I was wanting to look at some shirts."

"We have a good selection," she smiled and Jack's heart was won forever. From that day, Saturday after Saturday, Jack made his way to Stirling, sometimes walking both ways just to have a few words with Elizabeth.

"My goodness," Mrs Lafferty said to him one day, "you must have enough socks and hankies to start a shop of your own!"

Jack blushed and tried to stammer some excuse for his frequent trips to Stirling. Mrs Lafferty shrugged her shoulders. "Off with you, Jack," she smiled knowingly, "I hope the lass is worth all this walking."

Some weeks later Jack plucked up the courage to ask Elizabeth to go for a walk with him. When she said yes he couldn't believe his luck. As they walked she told him that the severe-looking woman he had seen in the shop that day was her Aunt Vera. She owned the shop and had looked after her since she was a small child. Her parents had died in a flu epidemic. Her aunt, who had never married, brought her up lacking nothing, but with little warmth. At best she was a cold, rather severe woman doing her duty.

As the months went by Jack and Elizabeth grew closer, while Aunt Vera tried everything she could to split them up. "You can do better than a coal miner," she would say to Elizabeth, "and an Irish catholic at that! To make it things worse, one day you will own this shop. I want you to stop seeing this Irishman."

But they loved each other and one day they stood beside the priest and were married, without the Aunt's blessing. She told Elizabeth she never wanted to see or hear anything about her again.

So the young couple moved to Loadie and made their home in one of the miner's cottages.

It took Elizabeth some time to get used to life in the village. Everything centred around the mine. Even the village shop was owned by the mine owners. The women moaned about the price of food in comparison to Stirling. They had no choice but to buy there. To try and compensate, each household grew their own vegetables in their own little bit of garden. Elizabeth was no exception, but to the amusement of the villager ladies she also found room to grow her favourite flowers.

"You can't eat them," they would laugh. But when they were in bloom they were thrilled to receive a bunch from Elizabeth for some special day in their humdrum lives.

Mrs Lafferty was Elizabeth's great help in that first year. She took Elizabeth under her wing, doing the same as she had done for Jack. It was to Mrs Lafferty that Elizabeth ran with the news that she was expecting a baby.

"You must take care of yourself," she advised. "You are such a little thing. I hope everything goes well for you."

On a cold February night Jack ran for Mrs Lafferty. "Elizabeth is in labour—please come quickly!"

"But she is not due till next month … Jack, go to the pub and get someone to bring the doctor!"

Hours later the Doctor, with the help of Mrs Lafferty, delivered Elizabeth and Jack's little daughter. Jack, pale faced, entered the room.

"Are they all right?" he asked the Doctor, holding on to the door for support.

"Yes, they are both fine," the Doctor reassured him. "You have a perfect little girl even though she is small. But Elizabeth has had a hard time. I don't think she should have more family—we were lucky this time to save mother and baby."

It took Elizabeth a long time to get over the birth of her daughter who they called Bridget. She went about looking pale and Jack grew more and more miserable blaming himself, but after a year Elizabeth picked p and became her old self, delighting in her daughter.

Two years passed and one day, when Jack home from work, he sensed that something was wrong with Elizabeth. When he questioned her she just smiled.

"I am pregnant again. Please don't be angry with me."

"Angry with you, my darling—how could I be?"

"It was terrified that you would be angry with me … but it seems to me that it is God's will."

"We will pray that it goes well with you."

And so the second child was born, another daughter they called Elizabeth. This time, to the Doctor's surprise, everything went well.

The years that followed were happy ones for the little family. Work was hard and long for the coal was in great demand to fuel the many new steam engines that were becoming more and more popular.

Elizabeth took great pride in keeping their little home bright and shining. Visitors were always impressed—a cup of tea readily thrust into their hands, a tray always set with one of her dainty tray cloths; and when the mine hooters went, Elizabeth would change out of her black wraparound overall into a dainty little apron to meet Jack at the door.

When Bridget was nine and Elizabeth seven, the whole world changed for that little family—for their mother was going to have yet another baby.

CHAPTER 2

▼

The two little girls sat across the dusty road from their cottage. They had been awakened early in the morning by their mum moaning, then their Dad telling them to get dress quickly and to go for Mrs Lafferty.

Frightened and a little scared, they made their way to her house. When she opened the door and saw the two girls she knew something was wrong.

"Come away inside," she said. "I don't suppose you have had anything to eat?" The little girls shook their heads. "Mum was crying—I think she is ill."

"Come then, my bonnie lasses, sit by the fire and you can have a glass of milk and some bread and butter. While you're eating I will run along to see your Mum."

Jack met her at the door. "It's Elizabeth—she's gone into labour."

Mrs Lafferty pushed pass Jack. Elizabeth was drenched in sweat.

"Oh, Mrs Lafferty," Elizabeth moaned. "The pain is terrible—it was never so bad with the girls."

Mrs Lafferty did the best she could for her; then, going to Jack, she told him to get the Doctor as quickly as possible. "Now then, go up to the pub," she said, "they have a pony and trap—that will get the Doctor here. You go to Elizabeth and I will get the girls."

"We want to go back home now, Mrs Lafferty, we want to see our mum," the girls were crying.

"Now girls, your mum is not ready to see you yet. You know she is going to have a baby and soon the Doctor will be here." She paused. "I tell you what, I must go back to your mum, but you girls can sit across the road and I can keep an eye on you as well."

So the girls sat gazing fearfully across the road and with every moan coming from the cottage they clung to each other for comfort. Elizabeth was tearful. "What's wrong with Mum why can't we see her?"

Bridget ever protectful to her little sister put her arms around her. "Don't cry, Elizabeth, Dad will come out in a minute and take us to Mum."

Just then from the cottage came a load scream. Crows resting in a nearby tree rose into the air with raucous cawing.

"Oh Bridget!" Elizabeth said. "The crows are crying for Mummy!"

Their Dad came out. He held his arms out to the girls and they saw tears streaming down his cheeks. Their big strong Dad was crying—they couldn't take it in. Then he told them.

"Your Mum has gone, your beautiful Mum has gone."

Mrs Lafferty came out carrying a baby. "This is your little brother. We must all try to be brave for him." She smiled sadly at the girls. "Come girls, you must come to stay with me for a while—this has been a sad, sad day."

Their stay with the kindly Mrs Lafferty lasted a year. They had moved back to stay with their father after a few weeks, but there was no end to his grief. He blamed himself for Elizabeth's death and sought solace in drink.

Cousins of Jack who had come from Ireland for the funeral realised that for Mrs Lafferty, nearly crippled with arthritis, was feeling it more and more difficult to look after a young baby, so they persuaded Jack to let them take the baby back to Ireland with them.

Mrs Lafferty did her best looking after Jack and told the girls that Jack showed little interest in anything; he went to work and sometimes went to the pub straight afterwards.

One day Father Michael MacQueen, a priest from Stirling, came to visit them. He shook his head when he saw Mrs Lafferty trying to cope with mountains of washing and cooking a meal.

"This can't go on," he said. "It's not fair on you or the children. I know of a convent in Fife that will take the children in to board. They would be well looked after by the Nuns and they would get their schooling there. Jack would only have to pay a small fee."

Mrs Lafferty shook her head dubiously. "I don't know, Father, I would hate to think they might be unhappy. After all, all their friends are here."

Father Mac Queen overruled this. "Nonsense," he said, "I will have a word with Jack."

Within a week the girls were bidding tearful farewells to their father and Mrs Lafferty.

The girls sat silently on the long journey. Father Mac Queen accompanied them. Elizabeth sat tightly cuddling a rag doll.

"What's that dolly's name?" asked Father MacQueen.

"Mary Ann," said Elizabeth, her eyes filling with tears.

"My Mum made it for me. I have it with me always."

They arrived at the convent. A tall wall surrounded it, and a large wooden door was set into the wall. Father MacQueen pressed the bell set into the door and a loud clanging came from inside. A panel at the top of the door was pushed aside and a face peered at them.

"It is you, Father!"

The door was opened wide to let them enter. A nun stood before them.

"This is Sister Maria," said Father MacQueen.

Sister Maria had a happy smiling face. She rested her hand gently on the girls' shoulders.

"You must be tired, children. I will take you to Mother Superior. Then you can rest a little before being shown around."

Father MacQueen excused himself. "I must go now, Sister. I have duties to do before heading back." He turned to the girls. "I assure you, you will be happy here, children. Be good—I will see you in four weeks."

The girls were sad to see him go. It seemed as if everyone they cared for were leaving them. The girls followed Sister Maria along what seemed to Bridget a long grey endless corridor. 'I don't think I like this place,' she thought to herself. Everything seemed so gloomy.

Sister Maria stopped outside a door. After a gentle tap a soft voice said, "Enter."

It was a large room and the setting sun streaming in the window made it seem warm and friendly. Mother Superior was seated at a large desk in the far corner. She rose as they come into the room.

"So this is Bridget and Elizabeth," she said.

Bridget felt that she wanted to run to her; perhaps it was the gentleness of her voice that reminded her of her Mother. She couldn't explain, even to herself.

Mother Superior continued to address them. "We have ten other girls staying here, all being orphans. You know what that means?"

"They have no Mum or Dad."

"You girls are fortunate that you have a Dad who loves you. You do understand, girls, why he couldn't take care of you, don't you?"

The girls nodded.

"Now, all the other girls who come to be taught here don't live in—they are fortunate to have families." She turned to the nun. "Now, Sister Maria, will you please ask Sister Monica to show the girls around?"

Again they were ushered into the long grey corridor, and coming towards them was a nun in a dark grey habit, just as though she had come out of the walls, thought Bridget. "This is Sister Monica," said Sister Maria.

The tall, severe looking nun faced them. "So these are the girls from Loadie." She studied the girls without smiling. "I hope you have been taught your catechism."

The girls nodded and Elizabeth's eyes filled with tears, remembering her mother doing her best to teach them a religion that she herself did not understand.

"What are you sniffling for?" demanded Sister Monica. "You're not a baby!" Her eyes shifted to the doll Elizabeth was still holding. "What is that you are clutching?"

"It's Maria Ann," said Elizabeth, clutching her doll even closer.

"Give it to me! You are not allowed toys."

Elizabeth's little face grew defiant. "I won't, I won't! Mary Ann is always with me. Mummy made her for me special."

Sister Monica made a grab for the doll and Bridget, in a fury, lashed out at her kicking and screaming. "You are a wicked! We don't want to stay here! We want to go home." Goodness knows what would have happened, but just then a gentle voice spoke behind them.

"What on earth is going on here, Sister Monica? Please explain." It was Mother Superior, disturbed by all the noise.

Sister Monica had to explain about the doll, but the Mother Superior seemed to grasp the situation.

"I think that maybe we shall allow Elizabeth to keep her doll until she gets used to her surroundings."

Sister Monica glared at Bridget and Bridget knew that sister Monica would never be kind or fair to her.

There were ten beds in the dormitory that Sister Monica showed them into. Beside each bed was a cupboard for hanging their few clothes, and two drawers for their underwear and toiletries. Hanging on the end of each bed was a towel, and the only sign of occupation in the room was a pair of soft shoes placed neatly beside each bed. On the wall a large crucifix hung.

Sister Monica pointed to two beds at the end of the row. "That will be your bed. You will be given a uniform and underwear when we get your sizes."

"We don't need underwear," piped up Elizabeth. "Look!" she said, opening her bag. "My Mummy made us lots of pretty underwear."

Sister Monica almost sniffed. "All the girls who live here must all wear the same clothes—that includes underwear." She went on: "I will show you where the chapel is. You will go there three times a day. You are due to go there shortly; then it will be time for supper—and bed by eight o'clock. Do you understand?"

The girls nodded. They were so tired, all they wanted to do was to crawl into bed. The other girls started to come into the room. They took off their coats, hung them up and put on their soft shoes.

"Did you enjoy your nature walk?" asked Sister Monica.

"Yes Sister," they replied in chorus. Just then a load gong sounded.

"Come, girls, time for evening prayers," said a cheery voice from the doorway. It was Sister Maria. Elizabeth and Bridget were so pleased to see her happy face again after the gloomy face of Sister Monica.

The little chapel was beautiful after the gloom of the rest of the convent. The evening light shone through the stained glass windows onto the altar, which was covered with a beautiful white lace cloth. On each side a candle stood in a tall brass candlestick, while under the alter space was a large arrangement of roses. Along the walls were pictures portraying the way of the cross.

Sister Monica took the prayers and after the final hymn they all went to the dining room for a simple supper of sandwiches and a glass of milk.

The girls by this time were almost asleep on their feet. Sister Monica was waiting for them when they went back to their sleeping room, as the two girls called it. On their beds was a collection of clothes, their uniform and underwear.

"Now, girls, wash quickly, say your prayers and into bed before I turn off the lights."

Bridget and Elizabeth hurried as quickly as possible and Bridget was almost in bed when Sister Monica pulled her back roughly.

"Why are you not wearing your knickers, Bridget Ryan?"

Bridget was bewildered. "We never wear our knickers to bed, they are just for day time."

Sister Monica flushed. "You are rude girls—you must wear knickers to bed, in case you touch your private parts when you are sleeping."

"What does she mean?" Elizabeth whimpered.

"I don't know, but we better do as she says. I'm so tired, I just want to climb into bed and sleep for hours and hours."

It seemed to the girls that they had just fallen asleep when the gong sounded for them to get up get dress, go to morning mass and begin life in the convent. To Bridget each day was miserable. She missed her Mum and Dad and all the happiness that was shared in their little cottage. She remembered being in a temper with her Mum because she never had a new dress to wear to the school Christmas party.

"Now Bridget," her Mum would say in her gentle way, "we can't really afford new dresses. For remember, if you have a new one Elizabeth would have to have one too."

Bridget, still not happy, had stomped off to bed refusing to kiss her Mother goodnight. Bridget remembered waking up the next morning rubbing her eyes because she couldn't believe what she was seeing. There, hanging on the end of the bed, were two beautiful dresses. Elizabeth had gushed: "Oh Bridget, do you think an angle brought them?"

"Well I don't think I am an angel," Their Mother had said.

Their Mother stood in the doorway. "Up you come, girls, and try them on."

Their Dad, on his way to work his shift, had said, "You are very lucky girls, your Mum stayed up all night making them."

It was a long time afterwards that they found out that their Mum had made them out of one her prized possessions—a red chenille tablecloth.

When all the work had been done for the day the oilcloth was taken off the table and the red chenille cloth was put on it, and it made the whole room warm and cosy. Bridget remembered all this as the tears ran down her cheeks.

Elizabeth seemed to be settling in better than Bridget. She was dainty, like her mother, and her gentle nature soon made her many friends, especially with the girls who came to day school.

The sisters were so different in both appearance and nature. Elizabeth had her mother's large brown eyes and her fathers reddish brown hair, which framed her delicate features. Bridget's hair was dark, like her mothers, and hung thick and luxurious to her waist. But her most outstanding feature was her eyes—slate blue, almost black when she was upset; even at her young age a strong sense of character shone through. This strength was going to be needed in the years ahead.

CHAPTER 3

▼

Day followed day and Bridget's sadness never eased. Why did their Dad not come to visit them? He had promised he would, and why had dear Mrs Lafferty forgotten them and, to make matters worst, Sister Monica seemed to find fault with everything she did. The only highlight for Bridget was when Sister Maria took them out for a nature walk. This took place every two weeks and today they were going to walk through the forest looking for mushrooms.

Bridget skipped along. It was such a beautiful day. Autumn had come early. Their leaves were already changing to their red and gold. A frost in the night made the spiders' webs shine like silver. Sister Maria looked at Bridget racing around, her long black hair billowing down her back, her blue eyes shining. Why, she really is quite beautiful, she thought, so different from the unhappy child in the convent.

When they got back Sister Monica was waiting for them.

"Bridget Ryan and Elizabeth Ryan, change your shoes and your outdoor clothes and follow me—you have a visitor."

The girls followed her into the dayroom. The tall figure of a man dressed in an army uniform was standing near the window. It took the girls a few seconds to recognise their father.

He had changed so much in just a few months. He had become so thin and his hair, though still thick, had become almost white.

"Why have you taken so long to visit us?" Bridget cried.

She held tightly to her father, afraid he would suddenly disappear again. Jack put his arms around his two girls.

"I am so very sorry, I thought of you both every day. But so much has happened since your Mum died and I knew you would be safe here. I missed your Mother so much I did not know what to do with my life. I kept working at the mine and Mrs Lafferty looked after me. Then everything seemed to go wrong. The new seam of coal, which was supposed to last a year, ran out, and the mine owner decided it wasn't worthwhile keeping the mine open. After just a few weeks it was all closed down."

"But nobody would have any money when the mine closed," said Bridget.

"That's right. The miners all left the village to find work in some of the bigger mines and the village was nearly deserted. I couldn't go because Mrs Lafferty, God bless her, took ill."

He stopped talking and hugged the girls tightly. When they looked up at him they saw tears running down his cheeks.

"Mrs Lafferty died. She was buried beside your mum in the little graveyard at Loadie."

The girls were heartbroken. Mrs Lafferty was like a mother to them.

"It's not fair," sniffed Bridget. "Why is God being so unkind to us? And I hate it here, father, I want to go with you."

"I'm afraid that you can't do that. You see, I am wearing a soldier's uniform. I did not want to work in the mine again, so I enlisted. I volunteered to go to Africa. Soldiers are needed badly there. I will only be away for a year, and when I come back the Army will find us somewhere to stay and we can be together again."

The girls cried and cried when it was time for their father to go. It was Sister Maria who was there to comfort them.

"Come, we will go to the chapel to say a prayer for your Dad's safe journey to that faraway country and we will find books to tell us all about it."

But Bridget could not be consoled and that night she wet the bed. She had wakened in the middle of the night feeling an uncomfortable stickiness between her legs. When she reached down she found her knickers were soaking wet. Rigid with horror, she thought, 'Oh God, Oh God, I've wet myself!'

Slowly she eased herself out of her bed. She felt along the sheets to find out if they were wet. To her relief they were only slightly damp, but her knickers were really soaking, though her nightdress by some reason had escaped! She thought to herself, if I can manage to wash my knickers and put them somewhere to dry nobody will know that I am going without them all day. She made her way on tiptoe to the bathroom. Little lamps were left burning all night in case any of the girls needed the lavatory.

'I wish that was my reason for going there,' thought Bridget.

She reached the bathroom without disturbing anyone. There was a large pulley there, which was always filled with clothes.

"Nobody will notice my knickers drying here."

She had just taken off her knickers and was just putting them into the basin when a voice behind her said, "So, Bridget Ryan, what are you up to?"

Bridget turned—standing in the doorway was Sister Monica! All her life Bridget would remember the horror of that moment.

"You are a disgusting girl!" Sister Monica exclaimed. "I knew you were trouble from the first day you arrived. Move, girl, you will have a bath!"

Bridget turned on the taps of the huge iron bath.

"Not the hot tap, you will have a cold bath. It will be a lesson for you never to wet the bed again!"

"Sister, please! I am so cold. Can I go back to bed?"

Sister Monica ignored her. "Climb into the bath at once."

By this time the bath was nearly full and when Bridget sat down in it, it came very nearly up to her chin. Every time she tried to climb out Sister Monica pushed her back in.

Bridget stopped trying to get out. It was so strange—she began to feel quite warm. But of course she was warm—wasn't she cuddling in beside her Mum in bed? She heard a lot of shouting somewhere in the distance. Sister Monica was holding her but now she felt cold, so very cold.

"She is coming round, oh thank God," a voice was saying.

With great effort she opened her eyes. Sister Maria and Mother Superior were bending over her. There were tears in Sister Maria's eyes.

"Why did Sister Monica do such a thing? She could have died! I don't know why—I decided to open the bathroom door as I was passing on my way to the dining room to set the tables for breakfast and …"

Mother Superior held Sister Maria's hand in hers. "Bless you," she said. "It was the Lord's will that you opened the bathroom door when you did."

"I think this child would have died with the cold. She must have been terrified of Sister Monica. As it is, she will need careful nursing for the next few days."

"We must find it in our hearts to forgive Sister Monica. I think she has a sickness in her head. I have noticed that she was behaving strangely for some time. She has gone now—she will get treatment. The life of the convent was not for her."

Bridget was strong, and in a few days she was up and was back into the life of the convent. But she would never forget what Sister Monica had done.

The weeks that followed were quite happy. With Sister Monica gone Bridget felt as if a huge weight had been taken from her. So much had happened in less than a year; surely now, she thought, everything would be all right.

And so time passed. Elizabeth had made a lot of friends with the girls who came daily to school. Bridget was a bit hurt to begin with that Elizabeth did not rely on her so much, but she was also pleased for her.

Then it was February and tomorrow was her birthday. She would be eleven. I don't suppose any one would remember, Bridget thought. But she was mistaken—in the morning she woke to the girls singing around her bed! Elizabeth hugged her and gave her red ribbons for her hair. The other girls clubbed together to buy her warm gloves and that afternoon the nuns came into the dining room carrying a beautiful birthday cake. Bridget cried tears of happiness.

The next morning everyone was wakened with a noise of a storm. It raged all day. Lighting, flash after flash, lit up the sky. Gale force winds howled round the convent. "Don't be afraid, girls," Sister Maria said. "This is a strong building."

Just then the sound of the bell in the gate startled them all. Who could be out in such a storm? Sister Maria hurried to the gate. Standing there was Father Mac-Queen.

"Oh father, what brings you out on such a day? Come in quickly and get dried."

Father MacQueen towelled his head. "I am here with bad news for the Ryan girls. I got word from their Dad's commanding officer that Jack Ryan was killed in one of the many skirmishes in Africa with the Boers. Will you come with me, Sister, to tell the girls?"

Elizabeth cried and cried, but Bridget felt too numb to cry. She felt angry. Why was God being so cruel? What was going to happen to her and Elizabeth?

Father MacQueen tried to comfort them. The day before he had received a letter from the priest on the island of Fada in the Hebrides. He was asking if he could recommend girls for fostering. One woman lived alone. Her husband and two sons had been drowned when their fishing boat had turned turtle in a freak storm. The priest had suggested that she foster a child to help her through her grief. She was getting old and needed someone in the house with her. The other family who wanted to foster just wanted to give a home to a child. Father Mac-Queen thought it Devine providence that he should have had both letters on the same day.

He spoke to the girls. Elizabeth between tears showed a shaft of interest, but Bridget was sullen.

"I don't want to go," she said. "I just want to stay here."

"You can think it over. You know, Bridget, you can't stay here for much longer. You're eleven now and of course there won't be any money coming in from your father to pay your fees." Father MacQueen continued, "I will take you to Fada myself, but it must be soon, because I'm being sent to England to be Chaplin of a large hospital."

So it was decided after letters were exchanged between the Priests, that the girls would go with him to their new home in Fada.

CHAPTER 4

───────────── ▼ ─────────────

Father MacQueen looked across at the girls. They had started the journey early in the morning on their way to Glasgow to catch the boat to Fada. He hoped and prayed he was doing the right thing. He felt so responsible for them, and he wouldn't be around to help them if anything went wrong.

Father Morrison was the priest on Fada for many years. He would, he was sure, keep an eye on the girls, but he was getting old and in poor health, and there was some talk of him getting moved to the mainland.

The girls were wide eyed as they drove through Glasgow. The streets were crowed with people going to and fro from shops that lined the street, and in some of the shop windows were strange looking men and women.

"They are models," explained Father MacQueen. "Really, just like big dolls, they are made to show off the clothes."

Smoke was belching from tall chimneys.

"That is the iron and steel works."

"I don't think I would like to live here," said Elizabeth. "The smoke makes me cough."

They left the street behind and now they were gazing at all the boats.

"That big steamer called *The North Star* is our boat," Father MacQueen observed. "It visits Fada every week with supplies. Come, now, girls let's get aboard."

They were lucky with the weather the sea was like glass. The girls sat on the deck enjoying this new experience. Father MacQueen pointed: "Look, girls, at the seals."

"They are following us."

"Will we see them on Fada?" Elizabeth asked.

"They are beautiful."

"Yes, you will, they lie on the rocks around the island; not just seals but dozens of different sea birds."

Bridget wandered around the deck. Suddenly she felt a great sadness. Everything was so beautiful and she wished her Mum and Dad were there with them.

A voice spoke to her. "Why are you looking so sad, my dear?"

A lady was standing before her. She looked so different from anyone she had met before. Bridget thought she looked like a queen; she was tall with black hair piled up on her head and was held with a silver clasp. Her earrings sparkled when she moved her head and the skirt of her beautiful green velvet suit trailed on the deck. Bridget thought, 'I do hope it doesn't get dirty.'

The woman spoke again. "Are you going to live on Fada, my dear?"

Bridget found her so easy to talk to. She found herself telling her all that had happened since her Mother had died.

"I live on Fada too," she told her. "I come from a city in England, but I just love Fada; it is so peaceful and I come here to write. We may meet again, Bridget, it is a small island. I do hope you will be happy there."

With that she smiled and walked away, leaving Bridget happy again.

They arrived at Fada in the sunshine, the deep blue of the sea lapping beautifully on white sand beaches.

Father MacQueen smiled. He knew that in a matter of a few hours the weather could change, and that waves as tall as houses could hit the island, the wind so strong that it was difficult to walk; but never mind, the sun was shining today to show off the island in all its beauty.

There was a crowd of people watching the steamer coming in. It was a big event once a week on the island. The boat carried all the supplies.

There were times in the winter months when the boat wouldn't be able to make it with the storms, but the islanders were used to this and they always put by emergency supplies to keep them going, such as meat and flour and feeding stuff for the animals. Father MacQueen took the girls' hands and led them over to two women standing a little apart from the crowd.

Bridget looked at them. They were dressed almost identically with long black skirts and black shawls covering their heads and shoulders.

The younger looking of the two smiled at the girls. She has a happy face, Bridget thought. But the other woman stared at Bridget, no smiles from her and she looked very severe. Father MacQueen introduced the girls.

"This is Mrs MacInnes, Elizabeth. She will be your foster mum."

Mrs MacInnes reached out for Elizabeth and, putting her hand on her shoulders, said, "Welcome to Fada, my dear."

But when he introduced Bridget to the other woman, saying, "This is Mrs Campbell—you will be staying with her," she said abruptly, "Come along then, we must find Ian MacIntyre; he will take us home in his horse and cart."

It transpired that Ian MacIntyre owned the village shop and had his fingers in almost everything that happened on the island.

Father MacQueen wished them goodbye, for he was going back on the boat.

"I will remember you in my prayers, girls. When you get used to the island I think you will be happy here."

Ian MacIntyre made room for them in the cart among all the supplies he had collected off the boat.

Mrs MacInnes chatted on. "Call me Morag, and this is Maggie," she said. "You can't go on calling her Mrs Campbell. We live just one mile from each other so you girls can walk to school together. I will point it out to you in the village."

The village consisted of Ian MacIntyre's shop, the school and church and a few outbuildings. To the left of the village was the smiddy and further along there were sheep and cattle pens.

They arrived first at the MacInnes' house. It sat in a curve of the bay. It looked quite small, stone built with a thatched roof with some outbuildings, which probably housed the livestock, but the view from the lane was spectacular. It was a clear view across a wide expanse of sea, and on the white sandy beach a rowing boat was tied up.

"I use that boat to do a bit of fishing myself just around the shore," Morag said. "I catch rock cod and maybe flat fish as they live nearer the shore and they make a change from the fish the men bring in. You can come with me one day," she said to Elizabeth. "It's good fun."

"Will you stop the blethering, Morag, I have got a lot of work to do when I get home."

"Now wheest, Maggie, I am trying to make the girls feel at home and now you have Bridget to give you a hand."

"I have a shop to run," butted in Ian Macintyre, "so if you can say your goodbyes we can get going."

Bridget and Elizabeth hugged. This would be the first time they would be separated, and they were both tearful.

"You will see each other in the morning when you go to school," Morag said. "Maggie and I will go with you to see your teachers."

A mile along a narrow track they came on Maggie's house. It looked much the same as Morag's with the thatched room and the two windows facing out to sea, but here there was a lot of activity going on. Hens were pecking around the door, a dog was barking a welcome and from the field a large black goat was baaing. It was tied on to a pole with a long length of rope.

"That's Nannie, she gets quite bad tempered when she is late getting her food. That will be our first job when we get in."

"But Maggie," Bridget cried, "I am too scared, that goat looks so fierce—why do you keep her?"

"She gives good milk. I make cheese from it and I sell it to Ian MacIntyre. The same with the eggs and so between that and the wool spinning I earn a living. The fish that Morag's men give me for the help I give mending their nets I salt away in a barrel. Don't worry, Bridget, we will never go hungry and the house is warm enough with a good peat fire."

"What is peat?" asked Bridget, so used to the mountains of coal in Loadie.

"I will tell you all about things later. Come now into the house. I'm desperate for a cup of tea."

Maggie had to bow her head going into the house for the entrance was low. They entered into the main room and it took Bridget a few moments to adjust. The room seemed so dark after all the sunshine outside. The fireplace dominated the room with clouds of smoke belching from it.

"Drat it," Maggie said, "the wind must be blowing in the wrong direction."

The floor was made of large slate slabs and beside the fire a pegged rug was the only bright thing in the room. Around the fire was an odd assortment of chairs, and a dresser in a corner housed various selections of dishes.

Maggie went to the fire and using the bellows soon had it glowing. A chain was hanging down the chimney with a hook at the end and on to it she attached a large iron kettle.

"Come now," she said, "while the kettle boils I will show you your room."

They mounted a ladder into what seemed to be a loft. The room was small and held two single beds, a washstand and chest of drawers. On the plain wooden floor was another bright pegged rug. But what drew Bridget's attention in the chest of drawers was a little case of snowdrops.

"Oh, how pretty. Thank you Maggie."

Maggie looked embarrassed. "Tis nothing. Come now, we will get our cup of tea."

Bridget suspected that the room that was to be hers had belonged to Maggie's two sons.

Poor Maggie, no wonder she had grown dour and bad tempered. Oh, I do hope she will like me, thought Bridget, and then she remembered the snowdrops that were put in the room to welcome her and she felt almost cheerful.

The next morning they were up and dressed early waiting for Morag and Elizabeth. They were going to take a short cut across the field from Maggie's to the school. When they arrived Morag was quite out of breath.

"Why, we have to go to the school this way I'll never know, it's not much of a short cut."

Maggie looked at Morag; there was concern on her face.

"You are a bit flushed, Morag. If you are not feeling well I can take the girls myself."

"Oh, it's alright Maggie, I have just been rushing about this morning. The men folk are due in tonight and I had a hundred and one things to do, but Elizabeth here has been a great help."

Coming on a rocky path a young boy appeared in front of them. He gave the girls a quick look and strode on in front of them, every now and then stamping his feet on the stones till the sparks flew from his tackety boots.

"Oh, so you have new tackety boots, John MacInnes! They won't be new for long if you treat them that way. Run along before I tell your mum."

The boy glared at Maggie. He was a handsome lad, tall and slim with the brightest blue eyes that Bridget had ever seen.

"That boy will be trouble with the ladies one day, just like his dad," Maggie said. She turned to the girls. "His dad ran away and left his mum to bring him up. She works all hours at the hotel just to feed and clothe him, so you girls keep well away from him; he is always up to mischief."

The girls had no problem with the schoolwork, as the convent had been very strict with their schooling. When playtime came the girls were shy joining in with the games. John MacInnes came across the playground. He was looking admiringly at Bridget.

"Would you girls like to play Chaser? The girls against the boys."

"No thanks," said Elizabeth primly.

"Yes I would," said Bridget and from then on she was accepted.

Elizabeth made friends with the quiet girls and that was the way it continued throughout their school days on Fada.

The weeks drew into months and soon the long summer nights arrived and with them much more work. The peats had to be cut and stacked against the gable end of the house. Maggie and Bridget were helped with this by kindly neighbours. Peggy's men folk, as she called them, brought baskets of herring, which had to be gutted before salting them in layers in a large barrel. Bridget hated this work. On the first attempt at gutting the sharp knife had slipped, cutting her fingers and the salt going with it made her cry. Maggie was sympathetic but strict, saying it's something she will have to learn.

Bracken and heather had to be gathered to fill the mattress.

One day she went with Maggie to the slaughterhouse. The smell was overbearing and she wouldn't go in. Maggie appeared with a pail of blood.

"What on earth are you doing with that Maggie? It's disgusting!"

"Not so disgusting, my girl, when you try the black pudding I'll make with it."

As usual Maggie was right—the black pudding was delicious and made a difference from the usual fish.

CHAPTER 5

▼

John MacInnes left school that summer. Bridget missed him. He went to work with Ian MacIntyre delivering groceries by pushing a handcart all over the island.

"I am not going to do this for long," he told Bridget when he was delivering groceries to Maggie's. "Next year I want to go to sea. I will earn more money and it will help my mam."

When Bridget told Maggie what he had said, she said, "Well, well, there is a lot of good in him. He does seem to appreciate all his mum has done for him."

It was some weeks after this that Bridget met him. She was taking the short cut into the village. It was such a beautiful morning. There were still traces of the beautiful sunrise touching everything with a rosy glow.

Bridget felt a strangeness inside. She wanted to run and dance along the road, then the next moment she felt like crying. She had been feeling like this for some weeks now and she knew that Maggie was giving her sharp looks.

She had gone to bed early, tired out as they had been busy all day carting seaweed from the shore to spread on the potato crop. Something had wakened her—the room was bathed in moonlight. She got out of bed and looked out of her skylight window. It was like magic—it was as bright as day and the sea shone like silver. She crept downstairs, frightened that she would waken Maggie. She ran towards the sea wearing just her knickers and vest that she had slept in. The sea felt warm as she paddled about.

I'd better not get my clothes wet, she thought to herself and hurriedly pulled off her knickers and vest and swam in the beautiful silver sea. She felt quite wicked and happy at the same time as the sea caressed her naked body. The moon disappeared for a moment behind the clouds and Bridget ran ashore pulling on her clothes. When she got to her room she dried herself quickly.

There was a strangeness in her body. Her breasts were growing and when she touched the nipples they grew hard. She remembered all this as she later walked along the road and, coming towards her, she recognised John MacInnes. She felt embarrassed as if he had read her thoughts.

They stood looking at each other. The footpath was narrow so they were almost touching. As Bridget tried to edge past she went too close to the edge and the next minute found she had fallen head over heels into a ditch. She struggled to get up, her face red with embarrassment. John MacInnes held out his hand for her.

"Are you alright, Bridget?"

"Yes, thank you," Bridget snapped.

They were now standing so close to each other that Bridget could see the devilment dancing in his bright blue eyes.

"Can I kiss you, Bridget Ryan?"

Bridget stood still. She felt her legs turn to jelly. When she tried to push past him, taking her silence as a yes he bent down and kissed her full on the lips. All sorts of emotions flooded her mind. She had wanted him to kiss her, yet she could quite easily have run off. She pushed him away and took to her heals, running for dear life.

Maggie looked up as Bridget raced into the house.

"What's wrong with you, girl? I thought you were walking to the village?"

"Nothing is wrong. I just felt too warm walking. I am going to wash my face."

Maggie, not quite convinced, nodded. Bridget seemed to have grown over the last few weeks. She was so attractive with her long dark hair hanging nearly to her waist, her long legs brown as hazel nuts. It won't be long till she leaves school, Maggie thought, and wondered what she would do on Fada.

"Will you take water out to that goat? She has been making such a noise all day—it must be the heat."

Bridget filled a bucket and had just laid it on the ground when a pain shot through her stomach. She gasped. She ran off to the outside toilet. She must have eaten something bad, she thought. When she took down her knickers to sit on the pail that was used as a toilet she found they were soaked in blood.

'Oh God,' she thought, 'what's happening to me? I am going to die! God is punishing me for letting John MacInnes kiss me.'

She started to run, brushing past a startled Maggie.

"What is wrong, Bridget? Good heavens, what is wrong with you, child?"

But Bridget kept on running. A sob had gathered in her throat, nearly chocking her, but she kept on running till exhausted. She flung herself on the ground among the bracken and then she cried and cried as if her heart would break.

From what seemed a distance, a gentle voice was talking to her.

"What is wrong with you, my dear? Do stop crying."

Bridget opened her eyes. It was the beautiful lady she had met on the boat when travelling to Fada that first day.

"Why, it's Bridget Ryan," she said. "My, you have grown. You are quite a young lady now. Tell me, why are you so unhappy?"

So once again Bridget confided in this lovely lady.

"I am going to die. Blood is coming from me. God is punishing me for kissing John MacInnes."

Elizabeth Armstrong was the name of the lady Bridget had twice confided in. She gathered Bridget in her arms and held her till her sobbing quietened. She felt such pity for this young girl who had been constantly told throughout her young life that her body was something to be ashamed of. Gently, she explained to her why she was bleeding.

"So I am not going to die?" whispered Bridget.

"No, you are not going to die and you're young and lovely and you must not be ashamed of the lovely body the Lord has given you. But come now, I will take you to my home and you can wash and have a cold drink."

They walked through a small wood and then on to a driveway each side of which was covered will all sorts of lovely trees and shrubs.

"Oh, it is so pretty, so many colours." Bridget was wide-eyed.

"You like lovely things, Bridget, and there is nothing more lovely than nature. That is what I write about. I travel all over the world making notes of trees and plants and the animals that live there and then I come to Fada to write my books. I love the peace of Fada. To me there is not another place like it in all the world."

They turned a corner in the driveway and there before them was the most beautiful house Bridget had ever seen. Even in books she had seen pictures of the homes of all the grandest people in the land, but none could compare with this house. It was like a fairy castle. Bridget had stopped with her mouth open.

The house was built of a reddish pink stone and was set on a rise in the ground. It caught all the sunlight which made the windows shine like mirrors. The centre of the house had two turrets and each wing jutting out from the main building had another. Beautiful lawns like a green carpet flowed down to the sea that sparkled in the distance. The lady took Bridget's hand.

"Welcome to Fada House, my dear." She smiled. "Do you know you don't even know my name? I am Elizabeth Armstrong and this was my father's house. My parents are both dead. I have a son about your age, maybe a little older, and one day it will be his. Maybe one day you will meet him. His name is William. He is at school in England, but he comes here for all his holidays. He loves it as much as I do."

Bridget felt as though she was in a dream. She wondered why in all the time since she came to Fada Maggie never mentioned this beautiful house.

They entered into a large hallway with a wooden floor covered with bright coloured carpet and a huge fireplace made with the same stone as the outside on the house. In the middle of the floor was a large round table with a huge bouquet of roses. Their scent filled the room. A wide staircase of white marble covered in a red carpet took them up to the first floor. Elizabeth Armstrong opened one of the many painted doors and ushered Bridget into a large bedroom.

Again Bridget just stood and stared. The room was so big! Her eyes were drawn to the bed, a large four-poster. The drapes, the palest green, matched the satin on the bed cover and the mountain of pillows. One wall was nearly covered with white and gold wardrobes, stretching from the floor and nearly touching the ceiling. Near the window a large dressing table had the same green satin skirt as the bed covers. The floor was covered with a thick green carpet. "Oh, I am so sorry," Bridget stammered, "I should have taken off my shoes."

"Don't worry about that," said Elizabeth opening another door. "This is the bathroom. You can have a wash."

The bathroom had the same green colours as the bedroom. Bridget stared. The bath was sunken into the floor: one had to step down into it. A rail was covered with fluffy green and cream towels and lots of bottles with silver stoppers were arranged on glass shelves. It was all so beautiful.

"Now you have a wash. I will give you some underthings and you can put your soiled things in a bag. You will find some in that little cupboard. I will leave you to it and go and get you a sandwich and some lemonade.

Elizabeth Armstrong's heart went out to Bridget. She was going to suggest that she gave her a pile of underthings but she knew the pride of the island people and knew she had to tread carefully.

Bridget, still in a dream, turned as the door opened and a girl not much older than herself came in carrying a tray with lemonade and dainty little sandwiches. "Her ladyship said she would wait for you in the Hall and walk back part of the way to your home," said the young girl, placing the tray on a small table.

"Do you work here?" Bridget asked.

"Yes," she said. "I have been here since I left school but my parents live in the village." She held out her hand to Bridget. "My name is Mary. Her ladyship told me your name."

"I would love to work here," Bridget said. "Everything is so beautiful."

"Well, maybe you will," Mary said with a smile. "Maybe we will meet again."

As they walked back along the road Elizabeth Armstrong asked Bridget:

"Will you come to see us again? We would love to have you visit and I am sure you would get on well with my son. He will be coming on holiday in a few weeks and sometimes I feel he could do with young company." She held out her hand to Bridget. "Goodbye my dear, I have enjoyed your company very much."

When Bridget got home she found Maggie in quite a state.

"Where on earth have you been? I have been so worried about you dashing off like that! You've been gone for hours."

"Oh Maggie, I have had the most wonderful time."

Bridget's face was glowing. She told Maggie about meeting Elizabeth Armstrong and about the beautiful house that was like a fairy castle.

"Why did you never tell me about it Maggie?"

"Well, I had no reason to; her ladyship only stays here for the summer months and when she comes she brings all the servants with her." Maggie Scoffed: "You would think that the people on Fada weren't good enough for her. She only has Mary MacIntyre as her personal maid and that mother of hers does enough bragging about it—you would think it was a special honour to be a servant. Just wait till I see her and tell her that she had to serve you. That will keep her quiet. Anyway, Bridget, go and get your jobs done. We will go tonight and visit Morag. It's a few days since I've seen her. I hope she is alright."

"Yes, I am dying to tell Elizabeth all that has been happening to me." Then she blushed. She wouldn't tell anyone about John MacIntyre kissing her.

Morag was sitting by a huge fire when they entered the cottage that evening. "Good heavens, Morag," Maggie said, "this house is as hot as a furnace!"

"I never feel it warm," said Morag.

Bridget looked at Morag. She seemed to have aged; her whole body looked so frail.

Maggie did not seem to notice the change in Morag as she chattered on. "Just wait till you hear the story Bridget has to tell."

"What story is that?" Elizabeth asked, coming into the room.

Bridget hugged her. "Oh Elizabeth, what an adventure I had today!"

She started to tell all that had happened. Elizabeth was puzzled. "Why were you running, Bridget?"

Maggie was embarrassed. She tossed and turned in her chair.

"Never mind about that Bridget, go to the bit when you met her ladyship Elizabeth Armstrong."

So Bridget told her story interrupted now and again with Maggie saying, "You never told them about the bath" or "You forgot about the white marble staircase", and so it went on till Morag and Elizabeth knew every detail.

When Bridget and Elizabeth went to make the tea Elizabeth whispered to her: "Why were you running?"

Bridget explained to her the way Elizabeth Armstrong had comforted her. "So that will happen to me as well?" said Elizabeth.

"Yes, but now you know, you wont be as afraid as I was. Maggie should have explained it to me but she was too embarrassed."

They drank their tea round the fire and Morag seemed happier as they chatted and talked about the old days.

"Do you remember the tricks we played on Bogie Roll?" Maggie was saying and they both went into fits of laughter.

"Who is Bogie Roll?" Elizabeth asked.

"Oh it's old Donald MacKenzie. He got called Bogie Roll because he chewed tobacco and that was the name of it. He still lives in the village; he has always been a bit simple but is as cunning as a fox. He knew everything that was going on."

"I remember some of the local boys saw him going into his toilet at the bottom of his little garden, a gae ramshackle place it was. Anyway, when he was inside the boys tied his door with a long rope and the other end to a horse in the next field. The horse took off after a smack on its rump, pulling Bogie Roll's toilet after it and there was Bogie sitting high and dry on his pail with all the world to see his bare backside."

"Now I have a bit of news," said Morag. "My sister Sarah is coming from America. I got a letter from her yesterday."

"Good news," said Maggie. "That is indeed a surprise. How long is it since she left Fada?"

"Oh, it must be at least fifteen years. You remember, Maggie, her and her pal went as nursemaids with a family from Glasgow. Sarah was the baby of the family and mum and dad were very upset at her going. But she settled down there and in all the letters home she seemed very happy. She married a well off man. He has something to do with the government and can't manage to come with her because he is too busy with elections or something. Look, here is the letter but it has a postmark of a month old. She must be well on her way here now because the boat takes nearly four weeks from America."

"Good heavens, Morag, there isn't much time to get everything ready! We will come tomorrow to lend a hand because I don't think you're feeling that well, Morag." She shot a worried look at her old friend.

"Well, I'm just a bit tired lately," said Morag.

"Right," said Maggie, "that's settled. Bridget and myself will be here first thing in the morning."

Good to her promise, Maggie had Bridget up and about first thing in the morning and as soon as the animals were fed they set off to Morag's.

In no time the cottage was shining like a new pin. Elizabeth was shifted into a little room off the kitchen to give Sarah a bigger room. Elizabeth didn't mind as she was enjoying the excitement of all the preparations for the visitor. Luckily Morag's men folk were still at sea so they weren't getting under their feet. As it turned out it was just as well they got everything done because the next thing Ian MacIntyre's pony and trap pulled up at Morag's door with her sister Sarah.

The whole village was agog: Morag MacInnes' sister arriving all the way from America! They were all dying to have a look at her and when after a few days Sarah went with Elizabeth to the village shop word soon passed round and Ian MacIntyre had never been so busy. They had quite a lot to comment on. Sarah was very elegant, tall and slim; she wore a very fine wool suit, no shawl but a little hat with a veil. But it was her voice that surprised them. It sounded to them as though she was talking through her nose.

She came one afternoon to visit Maggie. Gone was the wool suit. She had on one of Morag's working dresses. When Maggie commented on this she said, "I am here to help my sister. Don't tell her but her family asked me to come to look after her; she is a very ill woman. Morag doesn't know but the doctor told her mum there is no cure for the disease that is in her."

Maggie covered her face with her hands. "Oh my God, I knew she was ill and has been for a long time, but I never realised she was this bad. Poor Morag, my dear, dear friend."

The tears rolled down her cheeks. Sarah put her arms around Maggie.

"You and I must be brave for Morag's sake. She wont suffer any pain and right now she just seems to be tired all the time."

The weeks went by, Morag growing weaker and weaker and one morning, just as the dawn touched the sea, Morag passed away gently.

It seemed as if the whole island attended her funeral. The little church couldn't hold them all so they knelt on the ground around the church and joined in the hymns. Some of them sang in the islands language the sad Gaelic tunes.

From the church Father MacQueen led the mourners along the beach road to Morag's last resting place in the little graveyard near the sea. Bridget was afraid that Maggie would never recover her old self after Morag's death. She knew that she hid a lot of her sorrow in her abrupt manner. She knew that her grief over the death of her husband and son was so hard to bear that she had done her best to keep blocking it out with hard work and Bridget suspected that Morag had been the crutch she held on to, and now that, too, had been taken away from her.

Sarah and Elizabeth came to see Bridget and Maggie a few weeks after the funeral. Elizabeth came over to Bridget and held her close.

"What's wrong, Elizabeth?" Bridget, suddenly apart, demanded, looking into Elizabeth's tear-stained face.

"I am going to leave you, Bridget. I don't think I can bear it."

"What on earth is going on?" Bridget demanded of Sarah.

"I am going back to America and the men folk and I agreed that it wouldn't be fair to leave Elizabeth; she is too young to be left on her own when they go fishing for days at a time. So I am going to take her with me to America; she will have a good life there."

Bridget was stunned. They had never been apart, even on Fada.

Sarah talked to her in a soft voice. What she said made such a lot of sense that Bridget realised that if Elizabeth was happy to go it would be for the best.

Everything moved quickly after that and then there was Bridget and Maggie, standing on the pier waving farewell as the boat left, taking them first to Glasgow, then transferring to an ocean liner to take them to America.

Bridget felt she was beyond tears—she had cried so many since hearing of Elizabeth's departure form Fada.

For the first time Maggie put her arms round Bridget.

"Don't be upset," she said. "Elizabeth is going to a good life; be happy for her and anyway, it wont be long before you decide to spread your wings and leave Fada." She tucked her arm through Bridget's. "Come on, let's make for home and have a good cup of tea." Tea was Maggie's answer to all woes.

CHAPTER 6

▼

Bridget spent more and more time at Fada House after Elizabeth left. Some days she never went into the house but wandered about in the beautiful gardens. She was fourteen now and soon she would have to find work. She would have loved to work in the big house but as Maggie pointed out, her ladyship closed the house down throughout the winter months and departed with all the servants back to England. One day as Bridget was wandering round the rose garden her thoughts were far away, thinking of all the people in her life that she had had to say goodbye to, even a little baby brother who was somewhere in Ireland. It was strange, but she seldom thought about the baby; maybe deep down she blamed him for her mother's death. Sometimes in the night she would wake up sobbing, hearing again her mother's cries of pain. She was so deep in thought that when a voice spoke to her from behind a rose bush she jumped and almost fell.

"Oh, I am so sorry, I didn't mean to startle you."

Bridget looked up.

"You must be Bridget Ryan."

The tall good-looking boy held out his hand.

"I am William, and mother told me about you. She was hoping that we could be company for each other while I am on holiday here."

Bridget looked again; he was so like his mother. He continued talking: "I love Fada, don't you?"

He kept looking down at Bridget whose face was set with embarrassment. She was wishing that she had taken time to change and wash before she had left home, but she had left in such a hurry to get to Fada House that here she was with her old stained pinafore and her hair all over her face.

William didn't seem to notice.

"Would you like something to drink? Let's go up to the house. I'm sure mum would like to see you."

And so began a strong friendship between them. Bridget spent every spare moment with William roaming all over the island.

William told her about his life at university.

"I want to be a lawyer," he said, "but I would also like to spend my life on Fada. I wouldn't of course manage to do both but I am thinking too far ahead. I have got quite a few years study ahead of me yet. What will you do Bridget?" he asked her one day.

"I don't know. All I do know is that as much as I have grown to know Fada, I will have to leave to find work on the mainland."

The weeks of William's holiday passed quickly and Fada House servants had started the process of packing everything for the closing of the house for the winter months. William and his mother came to Maggie's to wish farewell. William shook hands with Maggie.

"Thank you for letting Bridget be my friend; it's the best holiday I have had here." He turned to Bridget. "I will see you in the spring." And leaning down he kissed her on the cheek. Maggie and his mother looked at each other and smiled.

Bridget missed them both terribly. She still went to wander about in the garden at Fada House but the nights were drawing in. On one of the late afternoons as she wandered about she had the feeling that someone was watching her. It felt quite creepy and she remembered one of the locals saying Fada House was haunted and that on winter evenings lights were seen in some of the windows. She turned to make her way home and as she faced the house she saw a light flickering in one of the upstairs windows. She was rooted to the spot but after a moment she was very angry. How dare someone wander about in the house, and as for it being haunted, she did not believe such nonsense. She moved quietly up to the front door. It was ajar. She tiptoed up the grand staircase not in the least bit afraid because she loved the house so much. She had just started down the corridor when a figure appeared out of one of the bedrooms and the light of the lantern it was carrying shone on Bridget.

The figure let out the most unearthly scream and ran towards the staircase, but in its hurry it toppled and ended up at Bridget's feet. It cowered down, crying at the top of its voice.

"Mother of God, save me, save me, don't let the thing get me!"

Bridget looked down at the figure at her feet and in the gloom she recognised the ugly old face of Bogie Roll.

"What do you think you are doing in the house, Bogie?"

At the sound of her voice he stopped raving and glared up at Bridget. He snarled up at her.

"I am supposed to be here! I look after it in the winter months. Her ladyship gives me a few pounds; nobody in the village knows this and they all stay away thinking its haunted and that way no damage is ever done." He glared at Bridget. "And what do you think you are doing here? Oh, I know—I have been watching you: you are trying to seduce young William! You are just a hussy. Oh, and I saw you kissing John MacInnes—I know everything that goes on in the village."

"You are just an evil little man," Bridget said.

Near to tears, she raced from the house with Bogie's laughter following her. She never went near the house again until she knew that her ladyship was in residence.

"You will need to find some work," Maggie said. "You are moping about the place."

This was true. With the winter approaching there was less work about outside. All the peats had been gathered and everything done in preparation for the winter months. She was in the village shop one day when John MacInnes's mother approached her. She was a neat little woman with faded fair hair; in fact, everything about her had a faded look. That is, until she smiled. It lit up her whole face and it was then that Bridget saw the resemblance to her son.

"I believe you have left school, Bridget, and are looking for work?"

"Yes, I am, but there is no work to be had."

Mrs MacInnes looked at her. "Well, you know I work in the Hotel and even although it's coming into winter, we are still very busy. Would you be interested, Bridget, in working there?"

"Oh yes," Bridget breathed, "that would be great."

"Well, you can come tomorrow. I will tell the owners that you can come for an interview, but remember the Hotel is four miles away so I will ask Ian MacIntyre to give you a lift. He will be going tomorrow with an order."

And so it was that Bridget started on her first job. The work was hard but she was happy. They would have liked her to stay in at the Hotel but she knew that Maggie would be lonely, still grieving for Morag, so every night she went home. Mrs MacInnes had given her John's bicycle and after a lot of spills she managed to ride it home each evening.

When she got home from work one evening Father Morrison was sitting with Maggie.

"Hello, Bridget, how are you getting on? Do you like working at the Hotel?" When Bridget nodded he said, "I am glad. I have just been telling Maggie that I am going away. I am retiring. As you know, I should have gone years ago. This island needs a younger priest."

"We will miss you, Father. You have been so kind to me and Elizabeth."

This was true. Father Morrison had helped them such a lot when they had arrived on Fada as frightened little girls.

"Come and walk a bit with me, Bridget, and we will have a little talk." They walked in silence for a while. "I hear that you have been seeing quite a lot of young William?" he said.

"Yes, I have, Father, we are good friends."

Father Morrison stopped and looked at her. "He is a lot older than you, is he not? And, remember, his way of life is so different from yours. When you are young that doesn't matter much. I am concerned that one day you may get hurt."

"Please don't worry, Father, he really is just a friend."

But Bridget remembered when she last saw William that there was shyness between them. They were no longer children running about all over the island.

"I will leave Fada when I am a bit older," she said, "but I will feel guilty about leaving Maggie."

"You must never feel guilty about that. Maggie has always known that one day you would want to spread your wings and leave the island. It's the most natural thing in the world. You have been a godsend to Maggie the last few years. Before you came I was very worried about her. I thought she would never get over the loss of her family." Father Morrison shook hands with Bridget. "Goodbye, my dear. I will remember you in my prayers."

With that he was off, just a little old man but with all the grace of God shining from him.

Bridget wiped a tear from her eyes. How many more times would she have to say goodbye to the people she loved in her life?

The next day at the Hotel Mrs MacInnes found her as she put on her uniform. "Bridget, will you do me a big favour? John is coming home tomorrow. He has been gone over a year working on the trawlers and I want to be at home when he arrives, but tomorrow night I am supposed to serve dinners. There is a big party booked in from some men's club."

Bridget, who had felt her face flushing at the mention of John's name, pulled herself together.

"Of course I will help out," she said.

Mrs MacInnes, a bit doubtful, said, "You will have to stay the night in the Hotel because you won't be finished till quite late."

"I am sure it will be okay. I will ask Maggie."

Maggie was a bit reluctant but agreed as she realised it was safer than her cycling home late at night.

Bridget, in the little staff room that was hers for the night, looked at herself in the mirror. She was wearing the black and white of a waitress and she had put her long hair up under a lacy little cap. This was the first time she had served dinners and she felt quite excited. She made her way to the Dining Room. Another two village girls were working in the Dining Room because it was so busy with the men's club.

"Don't be nervous, Bridget, we will help you. We have been doing this for years. Keep a smile on your face—it helps to get good tips."

The night went well. One of the men kept winking at Bridget. He was younger than the rest. Bridget didn't like him so she tried to ignore him. Passing his table he patted her on the bottom. Bridget's temper rose.

"Please don't do that again," she snapped at him. The other men laughed.

"She has you sorted out my lad."

The young man glared at Bridget.

At long last the work finished and Bridget made her way to her room. All she wanted to do was crawl into bed, she was so tired. She had just opened the door when she felt a hand on her shoulder.

"Well, well, Miss High and Mighty, are you going to let me in?"

It was the young man from the party in the dining room. There was a strong smell of drink on him. He pushed Bridget into the room and came in after her.

Bridget tried to push him back out of the door.

"Oh, so you want to play hard to get, do you?"

He gave her a push and she went sprawling across the bed.

"Just where I want you," he snarled.

Bridget screamed and screamed. She tore at his face and managed to get off the bed but he made a grab for her. She felt her dress ripping and before she knew it he was on top of her. She couldn't breathe. He was fumbling at his trousers with one hand and with the other holding her down on the bed.

"What the hell's going on here!" a man's voice shouted.

It was the night porter. He grabbed the man off Bridget.

"She was asking for it—they always are, these island girls."

That was the last straw for the porter who was an islander with two daughters of his own. "You young rat, we can do without the likes of you!" He caught him and literally threw him out of the door. He turned to Bridget who was near fainting. Her dress was torn and her long hair hung in a tangled mess. "Come in, child, calm down and sit. I will make you a drink."

"No ... I want to go home to Maggie, I hate this place!" She turned to the porter. "Thank God you came in time." With that she ran from the room, down the stairs and out through the front door. She never stopped running till she had put a good distance between herself and that awful man. Still sobbing, she walked along the road. It was so dark that once or twice she missed the road and landed in a ditch. A voice came to her out of the darkness.

"Who's there, can I help you? Don't be afraid, why are you crying?"

"I am going home to Maggie's, please don't hurt me," Bridget sobbed.

The figure came close to her. "Bridget Ryan, is it you? What on earth is wrong? Why are you out here in the dark?"

Bridget brushed the hair from her face and looked at the figure standing before her. It was John MacInnes. She held out her hand to him.

"Help me, take me home."

When they approached Maggie's they saw that the light was still on. She met them at the door.

"I never went to bed," she said. "I knew that this night something was wrong."

She put more peat on the fire and helped Bridget into a chair. She tucked a blanket round her and in no time a cup of tea was placed in Bridget's shaking hands. It was only then, when Bridget had calmed down a little, that she could say, "Now tell me, what happened to you tonight?"

Maggie and John MacInnes listened as she told them what had happened. John's face grew white.

"I am going to the Hotel. I will sort that guy out. He is not a man, just an animal."

Maggie sat saying nothing for a while, then turned to John. "When is the first sailing tomorrow?"

"Well," John said, "it will be with the first tide at six o'clock."

"Now John, go in the back and bring out the lantern and make sure there is plenty of paraffin in it. You and I have a job to do. We are going to the Hotel."

"Please don't leave me," Bridget wailed.

Maggie's face was stern. "You are safe here. Lock the door when we go. You can thank God that you are safe. With no light on the moor you could have wandered on to the bog. Many an animal had been lost in it."

It was very near dawn before Maggie returned. She never told Bridget what had happened at the Hotel but all the men form the club were on the first boat off the island and one of them looked as though he had had a good hiding.

John MacInnes came to visit the next day and for the first time Bridget had a good look at him. He was no longer the young boy who had left the island. He was always tall but he had broadened out. The blue eyes seemed to have gotten bluer but they were no longer full of mischief.

He explained why he had been on the road so late. He had sat talking to his mother till quite late and when she went to bed he felt restless and knew he wouldn't sleep.

"When you are on a ship for over a year it is difficult getting used to sleeping in a bed so I went for a stroll and thank God I did."

"I hope we haven't lost your mother her job at the Hotel," Bridget worried.

"Not at all. In fact, when we were talking Mother told me that an old bachelor uncle of hers had left her quite a bit of money and I have been sending her money since I went on the trawlers. He doesn't need my money anymore and I am saving to start some business of my own in a few years. She only worked at the Hotel to help out. She likes the owners. They are not responsibly for their awful guests."

When he turned to go he looked at Bridget.

"Can I come to see you tomorrow?" he asked. "I only have two days before I join the ship again."

Bridget looked at Maggie.

"Don't look at me!" she snapped. "You might as well, and I'll tell you one thing—I won't let you go back to work at the Hotel!"

So for the next two days they spent a lot of time together wandering around the old haunts and it helped Bridget to forget the horror of that night in the Hotel.

It wasn't till he was saying goodbye that he put his arms round her and gave her a hug. "I am always thinking about you, Bridget," and said and with a wave of his hand was gone.

After that Bridget prowled about feeling more and more discontented. Even her visits to Fada House did not bring much pleasure. Glowing letters arrived from America—Elizabeth seemed so happy she never needed to worry about her.

Then one morning, when she woke in her sixteenth birthday, she made up her mind to leave Fada. Maggie, ever sensitive to her moods, knew what she was going to say. In fact, Bridget was beginning to think that she had second sight into things. Like the time when she went to hang her favourite blouse out on the clothesline on a lovely sunny morning. "Don't hang it outside," she said, looking up at the sky where two or three clouds were to be seen in an otherwise blue sky, "the devil is riding the clouds and there is going to be a storm."

Bridget laughed at her but when she was on her way back from the village a storm struck and when she went to take in her blouse it had gone—blown into the sea, probably.

Maggie threw some peats on the fire and settled down on her usual chair. "Come and sit by me, Bridget, we will have a wee talk." When Bridget was settled, she went on, "I know you have made up your mind to leave and I don't want you to feel guilty about it. I must have seemed very hard and uncaring to you when you first came to me, but it's just that I am not able to show my feelings. It's just the way I was brought up." When Bridget went to interrupt her, she said, "No, now child, let me have my say. Father Morrison knew how near I came to a breakdown when I lost my men. I just wanted to die and when he suggested that I foster a child I wasn't for it. It was Morag, God bless her, that persuaded me. Over the years I felt as though you were my daughter and I have grown very fond of you. You have grown into a lovely girl, Bridget, and this worries me because without you knowing it you might attract the wrong sort of men."

"Never, Maggie, that man in the Hotel taught me a hard lesson. I will always be careful."

Maggie patted her hand.

"Well, they say that something good comes out of something bad. Well now, there is something else, Bridget. I have made a will. I don't have much to leave but this cottage will be yours and everything else that is left after funeral expenses. I have sorted all that out with the priest."

"Maggie please, please don't talk like that," Bridget, near to tears, implored her. Maggie shrugged back to her old stern self.

"Well, now that's sorted out, we will need to talk about where you will stay when the boat takes you to Glasgow. You will have enough money to last you a few days till you find work."

So everything was settled and when the boat came to the island the following week Bridget was on it. Maggie walked to the pier with her and before leaving the house she handed Bridget a package wrapped in canvas.

"It's a filleting knife, a good one. It may come in handy."

There were no tears when they parted but Bridget saw her standing on the pier, a sad figure till the boat sailed out of sight.

CHAPTER 7

▼

Bridget felt deadbeat; she had been walking the streets of Glasgow for ages looking for a cheap room. The ones she had seen were far beyond her means. She was excited and frightened at the same time with all the bustle and noise of the city. She decided to go into one of the many tearooms for a cup of tea. She didn't feel hungry but she just longed to rest her feet. She sat near one of the windows. So many people were rushing about; a man on the corner selling newspapers and shouting the headlines trying to make himself heard above the noise of the traffic.

A cheery voice spoke at her side.

"Can I join you?"

Bridget looked up. A girl of about her own age, without waiting for a reply, was pulling out the chair opposite. She had the brightest red hair that Bridget had ever seen and a smiling face covered in freckles.

"Have you just arrived from the islands?" she asked.

"Yes, this morning." Bridget was taken aback. "How did you know?"

"Oh, we islanders stand out a mile when we first arrive. I am from Orkney. Where are you from?"

"From Fada. I have been searching for a cheap room."

"I think I can help you there. I'm staying not far from here with a Mrs Moran. I know she has a room. The girl who was in it went home to Skye. She charges three shillings a week and we are allowed to use the kitchen to cook one meal a day. I go to the markets at the end of the day and I get good bargains of food. Come in and I'll take you to the digs before the room goes." She laughed. "I haven't even told you my name. It's Rosy Brown."

"I am Bridget Ryan."

They shook hands.

"I think we will be good friends Bridget," Rosy beamed as they made their way to Mrs Moran's.

Mrs Moran, a stout woman, showed Bridget the room. It was pretty cheerless—just a bed, a chest of drawers and a cupboard, but it was clean.

"Have you got anything to cook in?" she asked. When Bridget shook her head she said, "Well, you get the use of the store in the kitchen but you must use your own pots and you will need a plate and cup and some cutlery. You will keep it in the cupboard there. Rosy will keep you right."

In no time at all Rosy had her in the shop getting her bits and pieces. She is just like a mother hen, Bridget thought to herself, but she felt grateful to her.

"I have a job in a biscuit factory," she told Bridget. "The wages aren't very good but it will do till something better comes along. Would you like to come and see the boss? I am due back there now; we work shifts."

"Could I leave it just now?" Bridget said. "I have got something to do tomorrow." She told Rosy about her mother's death in Loadie. "I would like to go there just for the day to visit my mother's grave."

Rosy looked at her with sympathy. "Well, you can get a Charabanc in the next street. It will take you to Stirling, but I think it will cost you about a pound."

Bridget went to bed early that night; she was so tired. A lot had happened since she had left Fada that morning. There was a small gas fire in the room but she didn't want to light it. She would have to be very careful with her money. She was grateful for the thick blankets on her bed and very soon she was sound asleep. She woke early next morning and shivered a bit with the cold and dressed quickly. She was on her way out past the kitchen when Mrs Moran called her.

"Are you not coming in for a hot cup of tea? The kettle is always on the boil on the range."

"Oh, I did not think I was allowed."

"Well, I don't begrudge anyone hot water. When you get organised you will have your own drop of tea. Meantime help yourself from the teapot. Rosy tells me you're off to Loadie. Finish your tea and I will take you to where the Charabanc leaves from."

The Charabanc arrived early, full of passengers, but she managed to squeeze in beside two girls wearing waitress uniforms. All the people on the Charabanc seemed to be going to workplaces and by the time it left Glasgow it was nearly empty.

It was still quite early in the morning when they arrived in Stirling. One of the older ladies who had travelled with her asked her if she was just visiting for the day. When she told her she wanted to go to Loadie the woman shook her head.

"But there is nothing there, my dear. It's just a ghost village. When the mine closed everyone left. Most of them went to the big coalmines in Fife. I believe the mine owners in Loadie helped them to get other jobs there."

"I know this," Bridget said and once again she had to explain her reasons for going there.

"Well, it is a good bit of a walk there and back, I can tell you. Why don't you ask Donald the Cart to take you? He is a kindly old soul and won't charge you much. That used to be his regular run, taking supplies to the pit there."

The woman was right and for four pence Donald the Cart, as he was called, agreed to take her to Loadie.

It was still early in the morning when they set off. It was a lovely fresh morning and drifts of snowdrops, the aptly named Heralds of Spring, showed in some of the gardens.

"So you are one of the Ryan girls?" Donald said, peering at Bridget from beneath the bushiest eyebrows she had ever seen. "Do you know that I gave your father many a lift in this same cart when he went courting your mother in Stirling? A fine man he was. Oh yes, we all heard of his death, but when your mum died I think a large part of him died as well. Your mum was a lovely lady. I took then to Loadie when they first married. I remember the cart full of these wee bits of furniture and your father so happy that he would burst into song."

They came in sight of Loadie when they turned a bend in the road. Donald stopped the cart and they both sat silently looking down at the village. No smoke rose from the few remaining chimneys. Most of the cottages were without roofs. In the distance the large wheel of the mine was silhouetted against the sky—a sad reminder of a village that had died.

Donald turned to Bridget. "I will come with you to your mother's grave to pay my respects, and then I will leave you. I will have a walk out to the mine."

It did not take them long to find the grave. A plain wooden cross bore the name, 'Elizabeth Ryan, My Dear Wife,' and the dates of her birth and death, carved out roughly.

"I will come back one day," Bridget said, "and I will put a good stone on her grave, a stone that will last many, many years."

Donald looked at her and thought what a good girl yet old beyond her years. He patted her on her head.

"I'll go now and leave you for an hour or two."

Bridget knelt by the grave and cried for a mother that she had known for such a short time. She walked down in to the village and stood looking at her old home. It was almost a ruin. She sat on the step at the door. It still had traces of the thick Fife clay that her mother put on every Friday. She went inside and looked around remembering where each piece of furniture had been placed. She closed her eyes; she could hear her mother's laughter as her father teased her about something.

She remembered going with her father to pick elderberries to make wine for the New Year. The trees would be laden with large chunks of juicy berries. It was always her father who made the wine. He took great pride in it; she remembered the strong pungent smell of the berries as her father boiled them in one of the large pots. They were then strained through a muslin cloth into a wide enamel pail. She would be sent to the shop to get yeast. She remembered watching her father spread the yeast onto a slice of toast and put the toast floating on top of the wine and then covering the fluid with a clean cloth. It was placed in a corner for nearly six weeks. Her mother used to get cross with him because he used all the sugar in the house.

"Well, Elizabeth, the sugar and yeast are needed to ferment the wine and you will enjoy a glass at New Year."

"Away with you man, you know I don't drink. I'll leave it all for you and your cronies."

Bridget was remembering all this as she stood in the middle of the floor looking at the desolate empty room.

She was glad to turn her back on it and went outside. She sat once again on the step looking along the road, which was nearly covered in grass. She closed her eyes again and remembered playing with the other children on a lovely moonlit night racing up and down the road singing:

> *Girls and Boys come out to play*
> *The moon is shining bright and gay*
> *Leave your supper and leave your sleep*
> *And join your playfellows in the Street*
> *Up the ladder and down the wall*
> *A penny loaf will serve you all*

She remembered her mother coming to the door shouting, "Bridget and Elizabeth, come on inside, its nearly bedtime!" and going into the warm house and getting a glass of milk and a piece of dripping.

She could still feel the happiness at knowing how much they were loved and how lucky they were to have such a good mum and dad.

Donald, touching her on the shoulders, brought her back to the present.

"I think you have been here long enough, lass. It's time we made tracks back to Stirling."

Bridget sat quietly all the way back and Donald, too, was quiet. He felt so sorry for this young girl.

It was late afternoon before Bridget arrived back at her room. She felt drained and tired. She was lying on her bed, not even bothering to take off her coat, when there was a knock at her door and Rosy's head appeared.

"Can I come in?" she said. She looked at Bridget. "You look done in. I don't suppose you have eaten all day."

When Bridget shook her head Rosy wagged her finger at her. "Now that's not good enough. I'm off to get some chips. You can make the tea. Go into my room—I have had the fire on and it's warmer there than in here."

Bridget smiled at her. Rosy, as usual, was full of life and bossy, but it warmed Bridget's heart, knowing that she genuinely cared about her.

In no time at all she was back with two bags of steaming chips. Bridget's mouth watered at the delicious smell and she realised she was terribly hungry. They sat before the fire and Bridget told her all that had happened. Rosy sat quietly listening.

"I seem to have done nothing but talk about myself," said Bridget. "Tell me about your life, Rosy."

"I try not to think too much about the past," she said. "I have told you that I am from the Orkney's. Kirkwall is a busy port. Apart from the herring fleets some of the bigger boats go further afield for cod and haddock. Then, of course, there's the boats that carry all sorts of supplies to and from the mainland, not that we had much to do with the boats. They had there own crews for loading and unloading. My stepfather took me out of school when I was barely twelve to stand on the pier helping the women carrying the gut buckets."

"What are gut buckets?" Bridget asked.

"I'll tell you about that in a minute. My own father died when I was seven and my mother married again. I have got two younger brothers. I think my mother married to get some sort of security but that never happened. My stepfather was a lazy good for nothing lout; my mother took whatever work she could find to feed and clothe us and now, looking back, I think she was frightened of him. I don't think there was a day when I never felt the weight of his hand." She sighed. "Anyway, you were asking about the gut buckets. Well, the teams of women gutting the herring had a small barrel beside the big barrel that they were packing the herring in. Now, as soon as that small barrel was full of the gut you had to run to empty it into big containers and when it was full someone came to take it away. It was used as fertiliser. Anyway, for a long time that was my job and hard work it was for a skinny twelve year old. Because of my age I got paid at the end of each day, just a few pence, and my stepfather was there to take it off me every day. I was fourteen when I started the real job of the gutting. Mind you, you had to be quick but I'll tell you about that later.

"I had nothing. I was wearing a pair of my stepfather's old boots and even one of his old jackets and when I asked for a few pence I got a cuff on the ear. The women who followed the herring fleet were a great crowd. I was happy working with them and many a time they pressed a half pence into my hand. They knew all about my stepfather but they could not interfere. One day when my stepfather came to collect my pay I was a few pence short. I had put it all in my jacket as usual, wrapped in a hanky. I don't know to this day how I had lost it. My stepfather was furious. He ranted and raved, then pushed me so hard that I went flying banging my head on one of the barrels.

"Well, the women gathered round and helped me to my feet and then it was that the strangest thing happened. Not a word was spoken and with one accord they advanced on my stepfather. He was terrified! He tried to run away but they grabbed him and, lifting him up, they pushed him head first into the guts container! After a while they let him out. He had guts in his mouth, his hair—in fact, he was covered from head to foot! He ran screaming for help. One of the women, big Jessie who was a sort of leader among the women, came to me.

"Now, Rosy, I don't think you can go home tonight. Come with me, lass, and we will sort something out."

She took me to her lodgings, she collected clothes for me from goodness knows where, then packed me off to bed. As I was falling asleep I heard a lot of whispering going on and early in the morning Jessie woke me. She told me that all the women had a meeting and they had collected five pounds for me. One of the women had managed to talk to my mother and she had said that it would not be safe for me to go home and to try to get to the mainland for work and if I went it would be with her blessing. So all the arrangements were made by these dear people and that day I left on one of the cargo boats headed for Wick.

"I worked there for a while and then eventually I got fed up with the cold, gutting and packing the herring and so set out for the city and eventually I arrived in Glasgow." She smiled at Bridget. "So, Bridget Ryan, that's my story. Let's have a cup of tea and I'll tell you the good news. You have an interview tomorrow morning at the biscuit factory and with a bit of luck we will be working together."

The factory was just ten minutes walk form the rooms. Rosy led the way into an office. A fat-faced man was seated at a desk.

"Well, what do you want?" he scowled at Rosy.

Rosy pushed Bridget forward. "This is Bridget, Mr Rankin. I told you about her. She is looking for a job."

He came round from behind the desk and looked Bridget up and down.

"Well, I think we can fit you in. You will have to do something with your hair."

Bridget stepped back when he put out his hand to pull her fair back form her face. He gave her an oily grin.

"You can start right away. Rosy will show you what to do. We provide caps and overalls; make sure your hair is well covered."

"Don't worry about him," Rosy said as they made their way to get hats and overalls. "He is only the foreman. He has an eye for a pretty face—as if anyone would look at him. Mind you, saying that, there is one you will have to watch. Her name is Nelly. She thinks he is wonderful and she runs to him with all the stories."

The first day passed quickly and at the end of it Bridget's feet ached. The work started at an assembly line, packing the layers of biscuits into tins; some that were broken were put to the side and a girl collected them and put them into paper bags. They were sold in some of the small shops round about for a farthing. One of the women told her many a family survived on a bag of broken biscuits. She had winked at Bridget and said that they always managed to get a few whole ones into the bags. The weeks passed and with the bright summer nights they enjoyed roaming about the town looking into the shop windows.

"I am fed up looking," Rosy said one night. "A new dance hall has just opened down the town called 'The Locarne'. Let's go, Bridget, on Saturday night."

"But I can't dance," Bridget laughed. "Anyway, I don't have anything decent to wear to a dance."

"Right," said the ever-resourceful Rosy, "let's get to the flea market—we might manage to find something there."

"Yes, a lot of fleas!" Bridget laughed.

But as usual Rosy had her way and soon they were rummaging around.

"Some good things came in today," a cheery wee woman said from one of the stalls. "What are you looking for?"

Rosy as usual told her about wanting to go to a dance and having nothing to wear and very little money. The wee woman was sympathetic.

"Look here, these dresses just came in. A well-to-do woman brought them. She said she was clearing out her wardrobe because these things no longer fitted her."

Rosy and Bridget gasped when they saw the pile of dresses. They were lovely. A pale blue one caught Bridget's eye. It had a sweet heart neckline framed in a creamy lace and the same lace made a little bolero. The dress itself was made of shiny satin.

"I have never seen anything so lovely," Bridget gasped.

The woman smiled at the flushed face of Bridget. "It will be too big for you, my dear, unless you are clever with a needle."

"I am, I am!" Bridget said. "How much do you want for it?"

"Well, I could get three shillings for it."

Bridget's face fell. That was a whole week's rent money.

"Look," Rosy said, "I will pay half."

"You can't do that!" Rosy said. "Anyway, what about *your* dress?"

Rosy had been looking at a rich green chiffon that looked as if it was made for her. The woman looked from one to the other.

"Okay, you can have both dresses for three shillings, how will that suit you?"

"God bless you for your kindness!" Bridget said. She felt like kissing the cheery woman.

The girls couldn't get home to their rooms soon enough to start work on their dresses.

"We will have to look for cheap shoes; we can't wear boots."

So the next day off they went again and in no time in a second-hand shop they found just what they were looking for. Both pairs were much alike, black patent with a strap and button fastening.

Come Saturday night, they dressed with great excitement and made their way to the dance hall. They paid their money and followed the sound of music into the hall. They stood looking at he huge dance floor; large silver and glass balls hung from the ceiling, twirling round and round, making dazzling lights on the dancers.

They walked into the room looking for seats. It was pretty crowded and they had just sat down when two young men came up to them and asked for a dance. Bridget explained that she couldn't dance.

"Well, I will teach you. Come on, it's a waltz."

Rosy had already gone swirling away with a good-looking fair-haired fellow. In no time at all Bridget picked up the steps and started to enjoy herself. Her dance partner introduced himself.

"I am Peter and my friend's Johnny. We are both medical students in our third year." The four of them stayed together for the rest of the night and at the end they asked if they could see them home. "There is a fair at Glasgow Green tomorrow. Would you like to come with us? I am in the money for a change—it was my birthday and aunts and uncles have been very generous." Peter grinned. "They know that I am always skint."

Bridget looked at Rosy.

"Yes, that would be fun," Rosy said. "Will you meet us here?"

So it was arranged and with a lot of giggles they said goodnight.

The next day, true to their word, the boys arrived. They looked different in the daylight, much more serious looking than the night before. They explained that they were in the middle of pretty harsh exams and that this weekend was the first time they had let their hair down. Peter seemed to have taken for granted that Bridget was his girl for the day and the same with Johnny as he talked sixty to the dozen with Rosy. The fair took over a huge park. There were loads of things to do. Bridget, rolling a penny at one of the stalls, was thrilled when it landed on a two-shilling square. "Come on everyone, I'll treat you to a ride on the Big Wheel."

There was squealing and yelling as the wheel whirled them round and round. Peter put his arm round Bridget and hugged her close and she didn't pull away from him. She was quite happy with the comfort it gave her. They had a wonderful day. Rosy and Johnny walked ahead, arms around each other on the way home. Peter held Bridget's hand and when they reached home he bent down to kiss her. She moved her head away.

"I'm sorry, have I offended you?" Peter's face was troubled.

"No, you haven't. I'm sorry, Peter, it's me. I just don't want anyone getting too close." She couldn't explain to him that when he tried to kiss her she had a flashback to the awful man in the Hotel who had tried to rape her. "I had a lovely day, Peter, thank you so much."

She turned and walked away into the house. Peter shrugged his shoulders. Well, that's that, he thought—a good-looking girl: I wouldn't have minded seeing again.

When Rosy came in she was quite cross.

"What on earth were you playing at, Bridget, walking away like that? I thought you and Peter were getting on well?"

"Oh Rosy, I'm sorry. Did I spoil things between you and Johnny?"

"Well yes, you did. He was going to ask me out tomorrow night but when Peter left he ran after him, so that's the end of that romance." She shrugged. "Oh well, come on—let's have a cup of tea and a good blether." That was Rosy—never in a bad mood for long.

On Monday morning they were late getting up for work and it was a mad dash getting to the factory on time. When they went in the foreman was standing talking to Nellie. He looked at the two girls. Bridget's face was flushed with rushing and her hair was escaping from her cap and just as Sister Maria had noticed years before, the foreman thought, what a beautiful girl! As the day went on he found one excuse after another to get close to her. At one point her made an excuse to examine something in one of the tins that Bridget was filling and he put his hand over her breast. Bridget leapt back.

"Stop that!" she glared at him.

"What did I do?" he stammered.

"You know fine," she said.

Rosy came along. "What's going in here?"

The foreman walked away, giving Bridget a hate-filled look. When Bridget told Rosy what had happened she said: "I don't know how he gets away with it! He tries it on with the young girls and some of them let him because they can't afford to get on his wrong side."

When things had settled down Bridget absentmindedly nibbled on one of the broken biscuits.

"What the hell are you playing at, Ryan?" The foreman was standing behind her. "Who told you that you could eat the biscuits?"

"I'm not, it's only a broken one." Bridget was so surprised at him yelling at her. "Everyone does it—we never eat whole ones."

"Don't answer me back!" he yelled. "Clear out, you are fired."

Rosy appeared. Her face was as red as her hair. The foreman stepped back, a look of fear on his face as this bright tornado very nearly pounced on him.

"You slimy toad!" she bellowed. "You are firing her because she wouldn't let you put your hands on her tits! Well, you can keep your stinking job because we are both off. Away you go and fondle Nellie—you are both well suited."

With that she grabbed Bridget's arm and to the accompaniment of loud clapping from the rest of the girls they marched out.

CHAPTER 8

▼

It was now three days since the girls had walked out of the factory and they had been all over the city looking for work. They were careful with their money, going to the shops just before they closed for the night and getting bread and veg cheap. It didn't matter that the bread was already beginning to go hard and the veg, though tired looking, made good soup.

Rosy was saying, "I think we might have to leave Glasgow for work and go to one of the smaller towns."

Bridget didn't answer. She was reading a letter that had arrived that morning. It was from Maggie, who had enclosed a letter from Elizabeth. Bridget read her letter first. She felt guilty that she had not written her since coming to Glasgow. Elizabeth's letter was full of all the things that were happening in America. She seemed to be leading a full and happy life there. Bridget then started to read Maggie's letter that told her all the news of Fada. She sat bolt upright.

"Good Lord," she said aloud.

"What's wrong, Bridget?" Rosy was alarmed.

"Wait Rosy, wait—I'll tell you in a minute." Bridget read again Maggie's news.

Apparently a body had been found in one of the caves on Fada beach. It was the body of a man. It seems that he must have been walking along the cliff top path when he had fallen into a hole and with a recent landslide the body had been carried down into the cave. The man had been dead for many years. His clothing, though rotten in many places, still had one pocket of his jacket pretty nearly intact and it was in this jacket that a receipt from Ian MacIntyre's shop in Fada was made out to John MacInnes for paying his grocery account.

"Yes, Bridget, it was young John's father," Bridget read from Maggie's letter. "Oh, the sadness of it, that poor woman thinking all these years that her man had deserted her and that poor boy growing up without a father. I was as bad as the rest of the Fada people, so quick to judge; he was such a good looking man and I think now that it wasn't him who chased the ladies but the ladies who chased him. It seems he was on his way home to his wife and son when he fell, clutching in his hand, the dried remains of which were found, a bunch of wild orchids—his wife's favourite wild flowers."

As Bridget read Maggie's letter the tears rolled down her cheeks. "Poor John," she said, and she thought again about that kiss he gave her. She read on:

"There was a big funeral and young John managed to be there. He is still working for the whalers but he has bought a boat and is doing it up whenever he is at home. He has to be admired. Your friend William had been on Fada for the last few weeks. He is always asking for you. His mother is somewhere in Africa.— Sincerely, Maggie."

Bridget smiled at the "Sincerely". Was there anyone in this world more sincere than Maggie?

"I wish that I had known someone like your Maggie," Rosy was saying, "but come on, Bridget, buck up—let's put our thinking caps on and decide what we are going to do about work."

They wandered the streets looking for any kind of work but could find nothing and their bit of money was slowly disappearing.

"I have an idea," Rosy said. "Why don't we head for a job with the herring gutters? I have a gutting knife and your Maggie gave you one."

Bridget thought it was a good idea. She had been taught well with Maggie but would she be quick enough? It was a different thing, doing it for a living.

"But you will learn and I will be there to help." Rosy was getting quite excited with the idea. "We will go to the second-hand shop as we will need clothes to work in."

Bridget was a bit dubious about going to the second-hand shops; admittedly, they had gotten lovely dresses second hand, but this was different.

Rosy as usual persuaded her and Bridget went into fits of laughter when she saw what Rosy was buying—thick woollen jumpers that came down to their knees, men's trousers, jackets and even caps.

"You just wait and see, you will be glad of all these things. Now we will have to think about how to get to the nearest gutters."

Bridget left Rosy to take over. After all, she had spent most of her life as a gutter. "I think out best bet is to go to Fairlie. It's down the Clyde. We could get a lift there on one of the gut carts. They go back and forth all day."

The next day they packed their few possessions and dressed in the men's clothes. They set off early to start to see if there was work going. Rosy was right as in no time they found a gut cart on its way to Fairlie. There were two sailboats anchored at the pier and the place was a hive of activity with groups of women busy gutting the herring, not once lifting their heads, their gutting knives flashing.

"Look how quick they are, Rosy! I will never be as quick as that."

"Oh yes, you will. The quicker you are the more money you make."

Bridget looked around. All the women were dressed as they were—in men's clothing, because, as usual, Rosy was right. It was bitterly cold standing on the pier with a cold east wind blowing; they would have been frozen in women's clothes and, not only that, if they had loose clothing on it would get in the way of the gutters' knives.

The man who seemed to be in charge came up to them. "Looking for work, girls?" When they nodded, he said, "Well, they work in three's, two gutters and one packer. You will have to find a third for your team."

A voice behind them said, "Well, girls, if you will have me I would like to work alongside you."

They turned round and a cheery elderly woman held out her hand. "I am Kate."

The girls introduced themselves.

"Have you been at the gutting before, girls?" Kate asked.

"I'm sorry," Bridget said, "I haven't. My foster mother taught me how to gut but I'm afraid that I might be too slow for you and Rosy."

"Not at all," Kate said. "I have been waiting to get on a team. I have been busy mending barrels and doing all sorts of jobs. Have you got somewhere to stay, girls?" she asked. When they shook their heads she said, "Well, I have got digs ten minutes walk away. Come on, I'll take you there. You two will be able to share a room and you will save a bit of money that way. The room costs about three shillings and six pence."

She chatted on as she led them away from the pier to a long street. Their lodging house was two stories above a fruit and veg shop.

"The shop comes in handy when you want something to eat at the end of a busy day. It doesn't take long to boil up a few potatoes and veg."

The landlady, used to the stream of gutters coming back and forward as they followed the herring fleet, showed them into a large, quiet room. It had two single beds, the usual gas fire, a chest of drawers and a rope. This was stretched between the walls, presumably for their bits of washing. Right along the lower parts of the wall were newspapers. Kate saw them looking.

"They are there to keep the fish scales off the walls. Some gutters aren't very careful. Right, girls, leave your bags and we'll get back to the pier. We can't afford to miss more of the day."

So their first day as gutters began. Kate and Rosy gutted and Bridget packed the herring in the barrels, as she was shown, with their heads facing the side of the barrel. Each barrel held nearly one thousand herring. They worked until it was nearly dark.

"Girls, you have done alright today," Kate said. "How about you taking a turn at the gutting tomorrow, Bridget, just for a few hours?"

Bridget nodded. She would have to start sometime.

"I know you are tired, girls, and all you want is bed, but that won't do. I have some soup left and you can share it with me along with a chunk of bread, and after you have eaten my advice is to get in supplies. Have you got enough money? If not, you can get a sub on your wage."

The girls did indeed feel better after eating and were quite happy to let Kate take them to the shops for supplies. The fruit and veg shop was a godsend. They bought a week's supply of carrots, turnips and potatoes. Just around the corner was a butcher's shop. They bought a cheap cut of mutton to make a stew and a pot of soup. Kate was also a godsend for, if it weren't for her advice, they would have tumbled into bed and wakened early next morning to start a long day on an empty stomach. As it was, they were up at daybreak, keen to start work.

The next day Bridget would never forget. The bitterly cold east wind brought showers of hail. There was no shelter on the pier and no matter which way they turned, the hail hit them in the face.

Bridget's first attempt at gutting was a disaster. Her hands were so numb she could hardly hold the gutting knife. When she slipped and cut the palm of her hand she didn't feel it and it wasn't until the blood was pouring from it that she noticed.

Kate came to the rescue. She rummaged in the sack she laughingly called her handbag and produced strips of an old sheet.

"Come here, lass. I'll soon get your hands bandaged up but in such a way you will be able to carry on gutting."

Bridget was in agony. The salt had gotten into the cut.

"Can I go and wash my hands before you bandage it?" Bridget asked, nearly in tears.

"No lass, the pain will go soon and the salt will clean the cut and you can be sure there will be no infection. Look around you—nearly all the women have their hands bandaged and the first chance you girls get you will buy a sheet. There is always white cotton ones about the shops. They buy them from the Hotels. Some of them are in holes but that doesn't matter, they will get a good boil and cut into strips."

So it went on day after day with Bridget getting quicker at the gutting and soon able to hold her own with Rosy and Kate.

Sundays were the highlight of the week—a whole day to do what they wanted. The boats never went out on Sunday but they left the harbour exactly one minute after midnight. The girls, after a long lie in, were up and about doing the washing in a sink in the back yard. Their underclothes were hung on the string in their room but the heavy clothes had to be left in a basket, and if the weather was fine the landlady would hang them out on the Monday morning or on a pulley in her kitchen. Nobody hung washing out on a Sunday. In fact, the gutting girls were the only ones who were excused for washing on a Sunday because it was the only free time they had. The landlady left a large tin jug of hot water outside each door. With this the girls bathed and washed their hair. Bridget had a struggle with her hair. Even although she wore a cap it was still matted with fish scales. She moaned at Rosy.

"I'll have to get my hair cut. It grows so quickly."

"I'll cut a little bit for you but I don't want to spoil it," Rosy said. "You are lucky to have such lovely hair. Just look at mine—it has a mind of its own and it doesn't matter what I do, it just sticks out all over the place."

"But Rosy, you wouldn't be the same if you had tidy hair."

At this they both laughed. When they had finished getting dressed they went out exploring. It was a fine day but the wind was still quite strong and as they walked along the street a gust blew a cap from a young man's head straight onto their feet. Rosy caught it and held it out to him. He smiled at Rosy.

"Thanks a lot. I thought I would lose it."

He was a good-looking man with dark curly hair and twinkling brown eyes. He was taller than the girls towering above them.

"Can I treat you girls to a cup of tea?" he pointed to a nearby café. "Just to thank you," added with a smile.

"For rescuing my cap?" He was looking at Rosy. "Well that would be very nice," she said, ignoring Bridget's dig in the ribs.

'I'm Peter Black. I'm a merchant seaman. We docked last night and are picking up a cargo tomorrow morning for the Orkneys."

"But that's my home!" Rosy said. "You make me feel homesick."

"Well, we will only be there to unload. We travel round all the islands."

The three of them sat chatting for a while. When it was time to go he shook hands, but he was looking at Rosy as he said that maybe they would meet again.

When he went Bridget laughed at Rosy.

"Well, you clicked there, Rosy. Talk about love at first sight."

Rosy blushed but she had a strange expression on her face. "Oh well, that's our day off nearly finished. Up early tomorrow morning for another hard week."

"Rosy, would you mind terribly if I left you to go home alone? There is somewhere I would like to go first?"

"Good heavens, Bridget, I am not a child. Of course I won't mind, and I have a good idea where you want to go. It's church, isn't it?"

"You could come with me if you like."

"No, I don't like. I do believe there is a God—don't get me wrong—but I have no time for all the bowing and scraping that goes on in churches. I'll have a pot of tea ready when you come home."

Bridget found the church in the next street. She was just in time for evening Mass and Benediction. This was the first time she had gone to Mass since leaving Fada. Her feelings were so mixed up about the church. She had known nothing but kindness from, first, Father McQueen, and then Father Morrison, not to mention dear Maggie whose faith had been sorely tried with the death of her whole family; but there was a deep-down resentment in her, not only against the church but sometimes she even questioned God himself about circumstances and people—her mother's painful death, her lovely mother so gentle and kind, then her father dying in a strange country, poor Mrs Lafferty who should have had more years on Earth, and then Sister Monica: would she ever forget the cruelty that was in her?

The Priest had started the Mass. Bridget blessed herself and joined in the prayers, but her thoughts kept wandering, and it was the Priest saying the blessing over the bread and wine that brought her back and she asked herself what deep instinct had made her want to come to Mass today.

When she arrived home Rosy had the tea ready as promised. She kept on talking about the sailor Peter Black.

"He was handsome, Bridget, wasn't he? Why on earth did we not find out the name of the boat he works on?"

The next morning Kate knocked on the door.

"Come on, girls, up you get. Let's make our fortune today."

"Fat chance," Rosy moaned. "At three and a half shillings a barrel it's not very likely."

The weeks flew by and in no time the month of November was on them. The herring catches were getting less and less. The herring, a fickle fish, seemed to prefer the deeper waters as winter closed in and the sailboats were not able to follow them. A new threat was sniffing at the sailboats' heels—there were a growing number of steamboats.

"I think we will head off," Rosy said. "Why don't we make our way to Aberdeen? I heard some of the gutters saying that there is good money to be made there. The steamboats are bringing in cod and haddock as well as herring from the deep water. I think myself that the day of the sailboats has gone."

So it was decided at the end of the week they would head for Aberdeen.

CHAPTER 9

▼

The girls decided to work the week out at Fairlie and travel to Aberdeen on the Saturday morning, and with luck they would have all day Sunday to look around in Aberdeen to see where they might be working.

They didn't take long on their packing and saying their farewells and it was early in the morning when they set out. They were half way down the street when they heard someone calling. They turned round, astonished. Running towards them was Peter Black. He came up to them puffing and blowing

"Thank goodness I caught you! I've been running all the way from the harbour. Our boat docked last night but it was too late to come to see you. I got your address from your boss."

Rosy's face was flushed with pleasure. "You never took long coming from the Orkneys."

"Well, all we had to do was unload. There was no cargo there for us to take back here. Now this is one of the reasons why I wanted to see you, Rosy. I got talking to some of the gutters and I mentioned you, Rosy. One of the older gutters gave me your home address. I went to see them. Your stepfather died a year ago and your mother has been trying to get in touch with you. She is missing you terribly and wants you to go home."

There were tears in Rosy's eyes as she listened. "I have missed mother and my brothers. My stepfather was a hateful man. I'm not sorry that he has died." She turned to Bridget. "I must go home. Will you come with me?"

Bridget thought for a moment. "No, Rosy, it's you life there, not mine. I will still go to Aberdeen and maybe I will give up the gutting and find work in domestic service."

Peter turned to Rosy. "We go back to the Orkneys just after midnight tomorrow night. I'm sure the Captain would not mind taking you."

Rosy and Bridget looked at each other. This was the parting of the ways. Maybe they would meet again and maybe not, but one thing was sure—Bridget would never forget Rosy for all her help and kindness. They clung together for a last farewell and Bridget walked away, leaving Rosy and Peter going in the opposite direction.

Bridget felt compelled to take a Charabanc. She wasn't up to cadging lifts on her run and it was early afternoon when she arrived in Aberdeen. Bridget walked down Union Street. The smell of the sea seemed to fill the whole city and never had she heard such screaming from the seagulls. She was getting queer looks as she walked along. She had forgotten she had on the old clothes for the gutting. She decided to make her way to the harbour as she wouldn't be so conspicuous there and it would be the cheapest place to get lodgings for the night. She would have to be very careful with her money. The Charabanc had made quite a hole in it. She was lucky—the first lodging house that she went to had a spare room. She changed quickly out of the old clothes and decided that after she had something to eat she would look for work. It would have to be a live-in job. She went to the nearest tearoom and had a plate of chips with tea and bread and butter. She was getting used to being without Rosy.

She was on her own and just had to get on with it. She found a notice in one of the shop windows: 'Help Wanted, General Work, Live-in.' She decided to try for it. The house called 'Sea View' was at the end of a row of substantial granite houses and a notice in the garden stated that it was a Guest House. She rang the doorbell timidly. It was answered by a tall, thin woman dressed in black. Her black hair was pulled back in a bun with not one hair out of place. Sharp black eyes looked Bridget up and down. "Yes?" she demanded.

"I have come about the work. I saw your notice in a shop window."

"You better come in," the woman said.

She led Bridget into what appeared to be the family room. A young man was seated at the table surrounded by books and papers. He was very good looking with dark hair and the same dark eyes as the woman. Bridget guessed he was her son but the woman made no effort to introduce him.

"Have you done domestic work before?" the woman demanded. "If you haven't, you wont be much use to me. I have eight people staying. I need someone reliable to do the work."

"I have worked in a hotel and I know how to cook and clean," Bridget stammered, aware that behind the woman's back the man was grinning at her.

Becoming aware of this, the woman whirled round. She glared at him and then turned back to Bridget.

"I'm sorry, you are not at all suitable. I was looking for someone older."

Bridget's face fell. She really needed to get this job. The young man spoke for the first time.

"Now Mother, you really need the help, you know—you aren't strong enough for all the work without help and this young lady seems strong and willing."

Bridget looked at the woman again. She seemed to look as strong as ten women and the son was getting round her with a load of flannel.

"You are right, David, as usual." Her face had softened as she looked adoringly at her son. She turned to Bridget. "Right, you can have the job. Now, what's your name? I am Mrs Wright. I pay five shillings a week with your food and board—it's very generous. Come on, I'll show you your room. You will rise at six and help with the breakfasts. After that you can start on the cleaning and at ten o'clock you can have your breakfast of porridge and bread and butter. After you serve dinners at six o'clock you can have the night off, but you must be in by ten."

As she was talking she led Bridget up a steep staircase at the back of the house. There were two rooms. One of them was used as a store and one was to be her room. It was even smaller than the one she had in Fada. There was a single bed with two grey blankets, two sheets and a pillow lying on it. There was a table with a mirror and a jug and basin, and a cupboard in the wall for her clothes. The light was from a skylight and the floor was covered in brown lino. In all the rooms she had been in, this was indeed the worst, but it was clean and she was desperate.

She woke in the middle of the night freezing with the cold. She got up and found the big thick jumper that she had worn at the gutting. She pulled it on and went back to bed. She was barely back to sleep when a knocking at the door woke her up again.

"It's nearly six!"

She pulled on her clothes, still half asleep, and made her way to the kitchen. At least it was warm there. Breakfast things were laid out ready to be cooked. Mrs Wright was stilled dressed in black but she did have on a small apron.

"I don't suppose you have an apron?" She handed Bridget a huge wraparound one. "You will wear that when you are cooking and cleaning, but you must take it off when you go into the dining room."

Bridget was desperate for a cup of tea but it wasn't offered. In a short time all the breakfasts were ready and the guests, or lodgers, as she never knew what to call them, were making their way into the dining room. So it went on throughout the day, Mrs Wright watching every move she made. David had come down into the kitchen and his mother dashed about to get him his breakfast. He smiled at Bridget

"My mother is determined to get me as fat as a pig."

Bridget looked at him. There wasn't much chance of that—he really was a handsome man though there was a weakness about his mouth. No wonder, Bridget thought, with the sort of doting mother he had. He was an insurance agent, he told Bridget.

'That's why I can have a late breakfast," he told Bridget. "I can't go knocking on doors too early."

When she finished work she was so tired that all she wanted to do was climb into bed, but first she must write to Maggie to give her new address.

After the first week she started to cope better and, instead of crawling into bed, she decided to go for a walk into the town. She was standing looking into a shop window when a voice spoke:

"Well, Bridget, you have managed to escape from the house."

She turned. David, smiling, had come up quietly behind her.

"Where are you going?" he asked. "I'm at a loose end tonight and if you like I can show you the town. I'm quite proud if it. I wouldn't live anywhere else."

They wandered down Union Street, then along by the harbour. At one point when Bridget stumbled on the cobbles he held her arm and he never let it go during the rest of the walk. We are just like a couple, Bridget thought to herself, and she blushed at her thoughts.

"I must get home," she said shortly. "Your mother was strict about me being in by ten."

"Well, off you go, Bridget—I enjoyed walking with you. I wont go home just yet. I'm allowed to stay out later," he said laughingly. "Could I meet you at the same place tomorrow night, Bridget? I did enjoy your company."

Bridget nodded, then she raced off, terrified that she would be late and that his mother would be waiting for her.

The weeks went by and if it weren't for David she would have left. His mother was a bitter, nasty woman, and found fault with everything. She had her cronies visiting once a week and she put on a big show in front of them. Bridget made the mistake of saying she could bake and one night when she was on her way to her room to get her coat—she was meeting David—Mrs Wright called her back.

"You are rushing off a bit early, aren't you?"

"But my work is finished," Bridget stammered.

"You still have fifteen minutes. I have friends coming tonight. I want you to do some baking for them."

Bridget knew it was hopeless to argue with her. She hung up her coat and started the baking. If I hurry up and make some scones and a sponge cake it will only take twenty minutes and I will still be able to meet David, she thought. Everything went well and once again she was ready to go when Mrs Wright hurried into the kitchen.

"My, you are in a hurry tonight! Were you going anywhere special?" When Bridget shook her head she said, "My friends will be here soon. Would you set up the table in the lounge? We are going to play cards."

Bridget was resigned. When she was free it was late—too late to meet David, so she made her way up to her room. She got undressed and climbed into bed. She went into a deep sleep and thought she was dreaming when she heard a soft tapping on her door. She reached for the small night light beside her bed. The handle of the door was turning slowly. Bridget watched, terrified. Then a familiar voice spoke.

"Don't be afraid, Bridget." It was David. "Don't be afraid," he said again, "I waited ages for you."

"Your mother kept me busy. I did want to meet you, David."

He crossed the room and sat on the edge of the bed and Bridget pulled the bedclothes up to her chin. He stroked her hair, which, without her clasp, was tumbled about her pillow.

"Dear Bridget," he whispered hoarsely, "you are so beautiful—I do love you."

"Do ... you really love me, David?" Bridget's voice trembled. "Do you want to marry me?"

"Course I do, my dear one, but we would have to get engaged first."

As he spoke he was gently pulling down the blankets. Bridget trembled as he cupped one of her breasts in his hand. With his other hand he slowly pulled her nightdress up over her head.

"Don't be afraid, Bridget, I wont hurt you."

But hurt her he did as he entered her savagely. He never apologised when she gave a cry of pain. It was over quickly and he straightened his clothes.

"I'd better go. Mother might check to see if I'm in my room."

Bridget, on her own, turned her face into her pillow and cried.

They no longer went for walks. David preferred to come to her room to make love to her. This went on for weeks. There was no longer talk of marriage but after her pestering him he gave her a ring. It made Bridget feel less like a wanton hussy but he would not let Bridget tell anyone—it was t be their secret. His mother was not to be told.

Bridget was black, leading the huge range in the kitchen when the front doorbell rang. She heard Mrs Wright's raised voice.

"A Priest!" she shouted. "No priest is coming into this house!"

"I have a letter for your maid. Does a Bridget Ryan work here?"

In a trice Bridget was drawn to the door and the priest said, "You must be Bridget. I am Father Michel from St Mary's. I have a letter from the parish priest of Fada—a Father MacAulay. He replaced Father Morrison who you would have known."

"Yes, Father, he was a good priest to me and my foster mother. He retired just before I left Fada."

"Well, Bridget, he left word with Father MacAulay that he was to keep on eye on Maggie and to look after her affairs well. Maggie left her will with him. I am so sorry, my child, but your foster mother Maggie passed away quietly in her sleep. I have a letter here for you form her. Are you alright?"

Bridget held on to the door for support. Dear Maggie, never to see her again! The tears poured down her face. "I should have been back to Fada to see her. I never knew she was ill."

"Well, I don't think she was ill as far as I can gather. It was a heart attack. She did not suffer pain and we should be grateful for that. Now Bridget, if there is ever anything I can do for you, just come to St Mary's."

Bridget walked past Mrs Wright who was still shouting: "A priest coming to my door and me employing a papist maid! What will my friends think?"

Bridget sat on her bed reading Maggie's last letter to her with all the little bits of news of Fada. The Fada estate was being sold. William's grandfather had died leaving huge debts as he had made bad investments. William, the heir to Fada, had volunteered to sell his heritage to help pay the debts. His mother had married and they had made their home in Kenya. Her husband worked in a nature reserve there. The house was sold separately from the rest of the estate but no one knew who had bought it, but Bogie Roll still looked after it. Towards the end of the letter Maggie spoke of how happy Bridget had made her and how much she cared for her.

"I am leaving you the house, Bridget, so that even though I may be gone you will always be able to come home to Fada," Maggie wrote.

Dear Maggie, she must have had some premonition of her death and, like her whole life, everything had to be left in order. The tears were streaming down her cheeks as she folded the letter. Mrs Wrights voice from the bottom of the stairs brought her back to the present.

"What are you doing up there, girl? Come down at once and get on with your work!" Bridget hurried down into the kitchen and Mrs Wright turned to her. "I have a good mind to send you packing. You never told me you were a Catholic! I wont have priests coming to my door."

For weeks this taunting went on but Bridget paid her little attention. She had much more to worry about as her monthlies had not arrived for nearly four months. She was never regular but now she noticed a thickening of her waist. Dear God, surely not this could not be happening to her! David had been showing a coolness lately, which she had tackled him about one day. But he made some feeble excuse and couldn't wait to get away from her. Bridget thought, what did I ever see in him? He is so weak, just a mummy's boy.

Another few weeks passed and now there was no doubt about it—she was going to have a baby. She had started to get suspicious looks from Mrs Wright, so strange she giggled to herself almost hysterically: I don't even know her first name and she will be the baby's grandmother!

She was standing doing the baking when Mrs Wright and David were having a conversation when she felt the room swaying. She came to on the kitchen floor and sat up, dazed.

"What happened?"

Mrs Wright was standing over her.

"I'll tell you what happened, you slut! You are pregnant!" Mrs Wright's face was purple with rage. "You can pack your bag and get out! No Catholic whore is staying under my roof."

Bridget struggled to her feet and felt the rage rising in her. She picked up a large bag of flour from the table. Mrs Wright, guessing what Bridget was going to do, tried to take a step back but she was too late. The whole bag of flour poured over her.

Bridget turned at the door and the last sight she had of them was David almost crying, trying to clean the flour from his mother.

CHAPTER 10

▼

Bridget pulled her coat tightly around her. It was bitterly cold. A north wind was blowing, bringing with it flurries of snow. She realised she had had nothing to eat so she made her way to a little tearoom. She sat cradling the hot cup of tea. Dear God, what was she going to do? What a mess she had made of her life. Maybe it was as well that Maggie had died—she would have been broken-hearted. She thought back to all that had happened since leaving Fada. I wish Rosy was here, she thought. She remembered the urgency she felt about going to Mass on their last Sunday together; how understanding Rosy was. A sudden thought struck her. I think that was the day that Maggie died! Much later she was to find out that that was indeed the day.

She finished her tea and walked aimlessly down the street.

"Hello Bridget—it is Bridget Ryan, isn't it? What are you doing out on such a cold day?"

It was Father Michel. He looked at her closely.

"You seem upset, Bridget. What's wrong—can I help?"

His kind words were too much for Bridget and the tears started to flow.

"Come now, Bridget, don't upset yourself. The Presbytery is just around the corner. Come and sit by the fire and tell me what is so troubling you."

The priest's housekeeper met them at the door. "Your lunch has been ready for ages, Father." She looked at Bridget. "There's enough for two."

"I don't want to be a trouble," Bridget whispered.

"You're not a trouble, child. Father is the trouble when he is never on time for meals."

Father Michel introduced Bridget. "This is Anna; she has been the house-keeper here for many years. She bosses us priests about something awful."

"Och, away with you, Father."

Bridget looked at her. She must be about eighty, she thought, and she had the happiest little face, pink cheeks and a cloud of fine white hair.

Bridget felt herself relaxing and she started to tell Father Michel all that had happened since her mother had died. He listened quietly and when she had finished he asked when the baby was due.

"I think another four months."

"And you have nowhere to go?" he asked.

Bridget shook her head.

"Well, Bridget, we have a home for women who are in difficulties like yourself. You can stay there until the baby is born. You help with the work in the parish and that pays for your keep. Maybe it's a mother taken ill with no one to look after the children, that sort of thing. I'm afraid, though, that a few weeks after the baby is born you will have to move on. We do try to find work for the mothers but we feel that we have done our best and then it is up to them to make a life for themselves. We can manage to help five women at a time—I'm afraid that is all we have room for in the home."

"Oh, Father, thank you! I just did not know where to turn."

Anna appeared with a big tray of food. She turned to Bridget.

"All the girls come here one night a week. We knit and sew for all the expected arrivals and we have a good blether and a cup of tea." She smiled at Bridget "Make sure you come now; we try to make up for the family you are all missing."

Bridget settled in quickly. The others were all about the same age as she was. They had all been let down by the fathers of their expected babies. They were kept busy but found great comfort in each other's company.

As Bridget's time drew near she felt more and more afraid. Once again she could hear the screams from her mother as she gave birth and the crying of the crows at her mother's last scream. She spoke to Anna about her fears.

"But you are strong, Bridget," Anna said. "It seems likely that your mother may have had trouble with her kidneys. This sometimes happens in pregnancy. I have helped in many, many births and I have seen this happen. Don't be afraid, Bridget, our prayers are with you. You will soon be holding a beautiful baby in your arms."

The winter had passed, snowdrops were peeping out among the grass, and the birds were singing a dawn chorus at the first hint of daybreak. It was as she lay listening to them that she felt the first pain. She was afraid to breathe; maybe she had imagined it. Then she gasped—there was no mistake this time, she was in labour.

The girls all wakened with her cry. One of them was pulling on her clothes to go for the doctor though she was still half asleep. Anna was sent for as her presence brought calmness to them. The pains were coming fast.

"You are doing well, Bridget. First babies usually take their time coming into the world."

The doctor was just coming in the door when Bridget gave a loud cry and the baby was born.

"You have a lovely baby boy, Bridget," Anna smiled. She gave it a smack on the bottom and he roared in protest. She wrapped him in a little blue blanket and put him into Bridget's arms.

Never in all her life would she ever forget the feeling she had when she held him that first time. She was so full of wonder at this tiny baby she had brought into the world. All the unhappiness she felt when she first knew she was going to have a child disappeared like melting snow.

"I am going to call him Jack after my father! How I wish he was here to see him."

"Maybe your mother and father *are* seeing him," Anna said. "I think your mother was with you. I have never seen such an easy first birth."

When Jack was ten days old he was christened quietly in St Mary's. Anna stood in as his Godmother.

"You will soon be leaving us, Bridget," Father Michel said. "I have been making enquiries about work for you. I would like you to go where there is a family. You would be good looking after children and you could bring up your baby with them, but I'm afraid that there doesn't seem to be anything. But we won't give up hope."

"Thank you, Father, you have done so much for me already and now it's time for me to make a life for my baby. I will be a good mother, don't worry about that, Father."

It was only a few days afterwards that fate once again took charge of her life. Father Michel came into the home and he was accompanied by a middle-aged man. "This is Mr Stewart Bridget. He is looking for help in his farm house. He lives there with his brothers."

Bridget looked at the man. He had a kind face and the bright blue eyes of a man who had lived most of his life outdoors. He spoke to Bridget.

"Aye lass, our mother died over a year ago. She was nearly eighty but she kept the house clean and always a meal ready when we came in from work. We miss her sorely. If you come to work for us, lass, you and the bairn would have a good home and we would pay you a fair wage."

"Thank you, Mr Stewart. Yes I will take the job. When would you like me to start?"

"Could you come with me today, lass? I can only manage to leave the farm occasionally. This is our busy time."

"But I will have to get some things for the baby. Can we stop in the town?"

"Yes, of course. I have the horse and cart outside and as we will all be living in the one house you must call me Sandy. My brother's name is Sam."

Father Michel stood at the door, waving goodbye. Bridget thought to herself: I have been so lucky meeting so many kind people. After a quiet stop in the town they were off. The farm was about five miles from the town. It was a lovely drive. The spring day felt warm. All around the fresh green leaves on the trees were sending out their own special scent.

Sandy turned to Bridget.

"Now I must prepare you for Sam—he is a bit strange. When he was just a bairn he fell from the hay loft." At Bridget's look of alarm, he said, "Oh, you don't need to worry about him—he is very gentle. It was his head that got it and there are some days when he seems to act like a child."

Bridget's eyes filled with tears. "Your poor mother, it must have been awful for her."

"Yes, and for my father. I think it must have hastened his death. He died when he was only forty and my mother ran the farm and brought us up almost on her own, except at lambing and harvest, when she got help in."

They approached the farmhouse on a track across the fields. It was a two-storey house built with the Aberdeen granite. As they entered the yard Bridget noticed how spick and span everything was. It didn't seem like the usual farmhouse because the outbuildings were a good bit away across a cobbled yard. When the cart stopped a tall man came out of the house to meet them. He was taller than Sandy but one could never mistake them for anything other than brothers. He stared at Bridget and his eyes opened wide when he noticed the baby.

"This is Bridget, Sam. She is going to keep house for us."

Sam didn't seem to hear. "What did you bring me, Sandy? You promised to bring me something nice?"

Poor, poor, man Bridget thought, he was acting like a small child. The next moment he was a man.

"Pleased to meet you Bridget, we do need help." He turned to Sandy again. "I have a good pot of stew on." He then started to tell Sandy what had happened on the farm while he was away.

Bridget was led into the spotless kitchen. A large range dominated the room, not unlike the one at the guesthouse, but there the resemblance ended. This room was warm and friendly. A large dresser filled one wall, two comfy chairs were on each side of the range and a black cat was lying stretched out on a brightly coloured rug enjoying the heat form the range.

"We will put Bridget into mother's room, Sam. Will you carry up her bag and the baby's things from the cart?"

Sandy took her up the stairs and showed her into a large room.

"Oh, Sandy, it's lovely."

It was facing east and it would get the first sun in the morning. There was a large double bed with a patchwork quilt in bright blues and greens and the curtains on the window picked out the same colours. There was a small tiled fireplace, which Bridget could see lit on a cold winter's night. A large chest of drawers and matching dressing table shone with years of polishing and two or three chairs placed round the fireplace told Bridget that this wasn't only a bedroom but a sitting room as well. Maybe their mother needed this space away from the worries of the farm. She spied a sewing machine in a corner; this was wonderful—she could make clothes for baby Jack.

She settled in quickly. Sandy was like a father to her but Sam's quick changes from man to boy took longer to get used to.

After she had cleaned and washed, she wandered the fields carrying baby Jack on her hip. It was a glorious summer, the fields full of wild flowers. These she took into the house and had them dotted all over the place. It made the men smile. She was a good cook and when they came in tired their food was waiting for them.

As the summer was drawing to an end she noticed a change in Sam. She would catch him looking at her in such a way that it made her feel uncomfortable. She brushed it to the back of her mind. She just loved working there and as the days passed into weeks and then months she felt as though it really was her home. The sun streaming in her bedroom window woke her most mornings but even when there was no sun the clear light, maybe because they were so far north, made her jump out of bed.

The baby was growing so fast. He was a good child, even when teething. He gurgled and smiled and when the men came into the house he would hold out his little dimpled arms to be lifted.

Everything was so perfect there, she thought. She'd never been so happy and hoped nothing would happen to spoil it. It must be the Irish in her, she thought, that made her think something like that.

Towards the end of September, when the farm work began to slow down, Bridget had made a cupboard full of all sorts of preserves and had started lighting the fire in her bedroom. We are just like a lot of squirrels preparing for winter, she thought. There was a time like this on Fada, she remembered. She had just put the baby down for the night when she heard Sandy calling from the byre.

"What's happened, Sandy?"

"Get hold of Sam—he is in the milking shed. Daisy is about to calve but she is in difficulty."

Daisy was their prize cow. Bridget raced for Sam. He understood at once. Carrying a length of rope, he raced for the byre. Daisy was moaning.

"What's wrong with her, can I help?"

"Bridget, we need a bucket of water and a cake of soap. Her calf is lying the wrong way. I am going to try turning it. The soap and water is just for my hands."

Sandy dipped his hands into the basin and soapy water, then entered the cow, trying to turn the calf. The sweat was pouring off him.

"It's no use! I'll try to get the ropes around its legs and pull it out."

He did this and nodded at Sam. The two of them pulled on the rope and suddenly there was aloud *plop* and the calf landed on the byre floor with Sam and Sandy falling on their backsides beside it. Daisy started to lick the calf that was struggling to get to its feet.

"It's a heifer!" Sandy shouted.

He whirled Bridget round the barn. Sam looked on and once again Bridget saw that strange expression on his face. The next day Sandy had to go to the town to get feeding stuff.

"Will you keep an eye on the calf, Bridget? I won't be long—I'll go straight there and back." He looked at Sam. "You will be busy mending the fence on the bottom field."

Sam nodded. Bridget busied herself about the house and when she finished she dressed the baby and went to the byre. She was stroking the calf when she heard a sound behind her. Sam was standing at the door.

"I could give you a baby, Bridget. I know what to do. I saw the bull with Daisy. That's what made the calf."

Bridget backed away from him.

"Don't be afraid, Bridget. You could have another baby just like Jack. Look at me, Bridget."

Bridget looked. He had moved away from the door and for the first time she noticed that his spare was open and he had his male organ in his hand.

"Please, Sam, please don't touch me."

"But I have got to, Bridget. You can't have a baby if I don't touch you."

Bridget's brain was working overtime. She had to reason with him, she had to keep him calm.

"Now Sam," she said. Her voice came out in a squeak. "It is too dirty in here. You don't expect me to lie on this floor. Let's go into the house where there are nice beds."

He stood thinking for a moment. "Of course, Bridget, you are right. We will go to bed in the house."

He followed close behind her, his organ still hanging from his spare. Dear God, please help me, thought Bridget. Her legs were beginning to turn to jelly.

"I will have to go upstairs with the baby, Sam. You go into the bed in your own room. I will join you there."

She thought for a moment that he wouldn't agree.

"Okay, Bridget. I will wait for you."

She dashed upstairs into her bedroom and shut the bolt on her door. To be extra sure that he wouldn't get in, she pulled and hauled one of the heavy chairs and shoved it against the door. She heard Sam's voice coming up the stairs.

"Come on, Bridget, why are you taking so long?"

He tried the door and when it wouldn't open, he started to pound on it.

"It's not fair, Bridget! Why won't you let me give you a baby?"

He started to cry. He was a little boy again. In spite of her fear of him there was sadness—that poor muddled up man.

She heard the sound of Sandy returning. She shouted to him from the window. Guessing something was far wrong, he came bounding up the stairs. Sam was still sitting there.

"She won't let me give her a baby," he cried at Sandy.

"Well, Sam, what do you want with a baby when you have a baby calf to look after?"

"You're right, Sandy. I will just go and see to her feed. Did you bring me something from the town?"

Sam was back to his usual self but Bridget knew that she would never be able to trust him again. She would have to leave this wonderful place that had been home to her for only a few months.

The next day Sandy ran her into Aberdeen. There were tears in his eyes when they said goodbye. He thrust an envelope into her hands.

"Here lass, this will keep you going till you find another corner."

"I know where I am going, Sandy. I am going back to Fada."

She opened the envelope. There were twenty-five pounds in it, a small fortune.

"I will write to you, Sandy, from Fada."

CHAPTER 11

───────────── ▼ ─────────────

Bridget stood on the deck of the boat. The baby was sound asleep in her arms and she felt tears gathering in her eyes as she approached the pier. She was home to Fada. Such a lot had happened to her since she had left the island a young teenager looking forward to the excitement of living in Glasgow. Now she felt she never wanted to leave Fada again.

There wouldn't be anyone to meet her this time, no Maggie or Morag waiting patiently on the pier for two little orphan girls.

She stepped off the boat and a voice shouted: "Bridget Ryan, is that you?"

It was Ian MacIntyre. She had forgotten that he met the boat on its once weekly visit to the island.

"It's good to see you, Bridget," he said, shaking her hand. "Is it a boy or girl?"

"It's a boy, Mr MacIntyre. His name is Jack after my late father."

Bridget was amused he hadn't seen her since she was a young teenager and here she was back to the island with a baby and he spoke to her as if they had met a few days before.

"You will be wanting a lift to the cottage?"

Bridget looked to see what means of transport he had. It was no longer a horse and cart but the luxury of a motorcar. "When did you get this, Mr MacIntyre?"

"Oh a while back" he said. "We have got to move with the times."

All the way to the cottage he talked about all the happenings on the island.

"Maggie is sadly missed. She had a lot of sorrow in her life but she was a brave woman and just got on with things. You will find the cottage well aired and enough peats to last you throughout the winter. Morag's men folk have been looking after the cottage for you. Maggie insisted that everything should be ready when you came home."

"But how did she know that I would be coming back to the island so soon?"

Ian MacIntyre looked at her. "Now Bridget, you know as well as me that Maggie had the second sight. You will have heard that the Fada Estate has been sold; it was a sad day for young William. But anyway, he only managed to come here for short spells—he is a lawyer now and he works in London."

"Maggie wrote in her last letter to me that the house was sold separately from the rest of the estate."

"Aye, that's true. Nobody knows who has bought it but Bogie Rolls still looks after it and every month an envelope comes for him so someone is paying him, but he wont let on who. He is a crafty character."

"What are the people like who bought the estate?" Bridget asked.

"Oh, they seem a nice enough crowd—they are from Ireland. They have built a lot of new stables. I think they could be doing something with horses—it could be racing stables."

They came into sight of the cottage and Bridget had a lump in her throat. This was home. Ian MacIntyre turned the car expertly in front of the cottage.

"You must be the only one on the island with a car, though I do remember the big house had some sort of vehicle."

"Yes, I remember that, but I think it was scrapped. Now this car—" He patted it with pride "—is an Albion. It will go on for years. It was John MacInnes that helped me when I went to Glasgow to buy a car."

"How is John?" Bridget asked. "Has he married?"

She found she was holding her breath waiting for an answer. I am a fool, she thought to herself. What does it matter to me?

"No," Ian MacIntyre said. "He never married. He has done well. He now has three steamships and I hear that another boat is being fitted out with oil burning engines. He is a hard working lad. I noticed that years ago when he worked for me pushing a barrow all over the island with the grocery orders." He helped Bridget from the car. "I might see you tomorrow, Bridget. You will be needing some supplies."

He gave a toot of the horn and off he went and Bridget knew that within the hour everyone on Fada would know that she was back and with a baby.

It was a strange feeling going into the cottage. Everything was as she remembered. The fire was laid ready to be lit, the oil lamps' globes clean and shining and the wicks neatly trimmed. She looked into the fish barrel—row on row of herring salted away. She smiled at that, remembering the big barrels with thousands of herring. Jack was yawning. "Poor little baby, it has been a long day," she said. "You will be sleeping beside your mum, wee fellow, till I manage to get a cot for you, and I'll need to get you a pram or go-chair. You are too heavy to carry back and forward to the village."

She lit the fire and after the baby was fed, put him into bed. She decided to use Maggie's room as it had a double bed and the baby would be safe beside her if she put pillows round him. She didn't bother to light the lamp. She sat on the rug beside the glowing peat fire instead. It will be so good for Jack to grow up surrounded by the good Fada people, she thought.

She woke in the morning with someone knocking on the door and then a voice with a strong Irish accent shouted:

"Are you in there, Bridget?"

She pulled on her coat and opened the door. A man and woman were standing there with a horse and cart that seemed to be full of people. The woman spoke to her.

"Bridget, you have the look of your father about you!" She dug the man in the ribs. "Will you look, Shamus, look at the colour of that hair."

"My father's hair was fair and if you look mine is quite dark," said Bridget.

"Oh, it's just the way the morning light was shining on it," the woman replied. "You see, my dear, it's been a long time—do you not remember me? I am your father's cousin from Tipperary. I took your little baby brother to Ireland to bring up as my own."

"Oh, I am so sorry to leave you standing on the doorstep. I am still half asleep—I only arrived yesterday."

"We know that—the man in the shop told us. We have been trying to trace you for months! We have been in touch with Elizabeth. The nice man in the next cottage gave us her address. She is going to try to get here. Did you know she has married an American?"

"No, I didn't know and I feel so ashamed that I haven't written her for ages."

The cottage was bursting at the seams with the big Irish people all talking at the same time. The cousin of her fathers was a big good-natured woman and she was so happy with all his family around her.

"You will be my second cousin, Bridget, but it will be nicer if you call me Aunt Mo. My name is Maureen but I never get my title, do I Shamus?"

Shamus shook his head at her. "Do you ever stop talking? Look at poor Bridget! I'm sure her head is going round."

He was right—it was all too much to take in.

"Where are you all staying?" she asked, keeping her fingers crosses that they weren't expecting her to put them up.

"Now there you are, Mo, you haven't told the poor girl the most important thing." He turned to Bridget. "We have bought the Fada Estate, or most of it. They wouldn't sell us the big house and the few acres of ground around it but we have enough. We are having riding stables built and we are breeding racehorses. We had good stables in Ireland but we got fed up travelling across the Irish Sea to race meetings. We wont have such a long journey from here. We heard about the estate being up for sale from a young fellow. We used his boats. His name was John MacInnes—he said he knew you."

Bridget looked around the room. Anything to change the subject. "But where is John, my young brother?"

Bridget looked and gasped. It was like looking at a young version of her father. He had the same colouring and already he was nearly six feet tall. But it wasn't only that—it was the way he stood and the devil may care laughter in his eyes. He was full of confidence for a fourteen year old.

"Can I give my big sister a hug?" he said.

Bridget reached out her arms for him, the tears streaming down her face.

"Come on now," Mo was demanding. "No time for tears. We have plenty of time to catch up. We will just have a peep at your baby. The man in the shop said you called him Jack. I'm pleased about that." She turned to one of the boys. "Go out to the cart and bring the things in. The man in the shop said you needed these things. They aren't new. He was going to give them to you but we Ryan's pay our way."

The boy appeared struggling with a go-chair and went back to the cart. He brought in a cot that was big enough for a two-year-old. Bridget was speechless. She put her arms round Mo and hugged her.

"An awful lot of crying going on in this house," her newly found young brother stated on his way out.

Bridget followed him out and saw him riding off on a beautiful black horse. He gave a jaunty wave and he was away.

"We love him dearly," Mo said at her side. "He has a wonderful nature. He is so easy to love. We must go now, Bridget. We have rented an old farmhouse till we get our own place built. It was more important to get the stables built as our horses are coming from Ireland in a few weeks."

Amid shouts and cheerio's they were off—her cheery, happy, Irish family! No airs or graces about them, yet there they were buying the Fada Estate.

The next morning Bridget was up early. It was a beautiful, crisp early autumn day. She built up the fire, made the bed and when the house was neat and tidy she put Jack in the go-chair and set of for the village. She needed very little—milk, eggs and maybe a bag of flour. She would do a baking tonight; one never knew when someone might drop in for a chat and a cup of tea. That was the way it was with Fada people, as with all the other islands. Someone had told her once that in England, if you called to visit, you would get a cup of tea but nothing to eat with it—not even a biscuit.

She walked slowly, enjoying every minute. She couldn't quite believe that she was here on Fada and walking with her baby son. She arrived at the shop and within minutes a crowd had gathered round her, looking and smiling at the baby. She knew that they would love to start questioning her about the baby's father. One sharp-faced little woman with a strong Glasgow accent was bolder.

"She doesn't look like you, hen, does he take after his father?"

Bridget ignored her and when she was alone in the shop she asked Ian MacIntyre who the woman was.

He sighed. "Well, I'm afraid we are going to have a few strangers staying on Fada. That woman's husband works on the boats. John MacInnes bought the row of cottages down by the pier. He did them up for the men who work for him and they bring their wives and families. Aye, Bridget, a lot of changes on Fada, maybe for the best and maybe not."

Bridget was deep in thought as she walked home. She seemed to be hearing nothing but John MacInnes did this and John MacInnes did that. "I want the old Fada to myself," she thought—where everyone knew everyone else. Then she remembered: "I suppose my family are just as bad. I am sure the locals are a bit annoyed at the invasion of all my Irish cousins." The day passed and Bridget settled into a routine. I must get a few hens, she thought. I could sell the eggs to the shop, the same as Maggie did, and maybe I could start knitting and sell to the shops in Glasgow.

But the thought that was uppermost in her mind was to visit Fada House. "I wonder if it is still beautiful," she thought, "or was it because I was just a child coming from a small cottage?"

CHAPTER 12

▼

Bridget marvelled at her Irish family. They always seemed so happy; after all, they had pulled up their Irish roots and settled somewhere completely different. They had four sons of their own and John, who was in every way their son. Their eldest, called Shamus after his father, was twenty; then there was Rory, nineteen, Matthew, eighteen, and Peter, seventeen, and, of course, John at fourteen. She was sitting talking beside the fire with Mo.

"You had your hands full, Mo, with all the boys. What a pity you never had a girl, Mo; she would have been a help to you."

Mo never answered and when Bridget looked she saw the tears streaming down her cheeks.

"Oh Mo, what's wrong?"

"Don't worry about me, Bridget. I am just a silly old woman."

"No, Mo, something has upset you. Was it something I said?"

She patted Bridget's knee. "It happened a long time ago. We did have a daughter. Mary, we called her. She was the most beautiful baby. She had the Ryan red hair curled round the loveliest little face with long eyelashes that rested like little fans on her cheeks when she was asleep. One Saturday we were all outside—it was a lovely day. The boys were racing about and Mary was sitting on the ground playing with the clothes pegs. I was hanging out some washing when Matthew came crying to me. He had stung his legs on some nettles and I was looking around for dock leaves to put on his sting. I turned to look at Mary but she was no longer sitting on the ground. We raced about looking and shouting for her. I ran into the house thinking she may have gone there, but no. There was a little burn at the bottom of the garden but it never held much water. Something drew me there and I found her, my little two and a half year old baby. It was her red hair I noticed first. She had fallen, banging her head; she was lying face down in just a little puddle of water, but it was enough to drown her. I think I must have gone mad! I don't remember much even to this day. Poor Shamus—he loved her as much as me but I just left him to it, sitting day after day in my room, not even bothering with the boys. I think about six weeks had passed when word came about your mother and how she had gone, leaving you girls and a new baby; something clicked in my mind and I think I surprised Shamus when I told him I was going to Scotland and that I might be coming back with Jack's baby son. I think he was happy that I had found something that would help. You know the rest, my dear. I wish we had been able to take you and Elizabeth but things were hard at that time and we couldn't manage to take you all. Baby John brought peace and some happiness back into our family—that's why we all love him so much. God does indeed work in mysterious ways.

Bridget found it strange that two or three times a week the whole family would descend on her but she was grateful for their company and they seemed to be happy crowding round the peat fire; and then, so typical of what she was learning, the stories would start, one trying to outdo the other.

"Come now, Bridget, you must have a story. You lived with Maggie long enough. She must have had some good ones."

"Well," Bridget began, "she did tell me the story of the Devil's Rock."

"Go on then, Bridget, go on."

"Well, there were these three men in the village. They were a bit wild. They would never go to church on a Sunday; instead they would meet not so far away from here behind a big rock. No one could see them from the road and there they would gamble with the cards. Well, they had been playing for a while when this man joined them. Can I join with you, he asked? Yes of course they said. So they started another game but they weren't happy and they started to quarrel among themselves and as the game continued the quarrelling got worse and worse. Then one of the men dropped a card on the ground. He bent down to pick it up and he saw to his horror that the man who had joined them had cloven hoofs instead of feet. They had been playing cards with the Devil. They raced home for dear life and never again did they miss going to church and never again did they play cards."

"That was a great story, Bridget! You don't think it was true do you?"

"Well, I don't know, but nobody likes to go past that stone, especially at night."

Bridget received a letter form Elizabeth, saying:

'Dear Bridget,

By the time you receive this letter (I know what living on Fada is like with the mail) I will probably be standing on the doorstep the same as what happened to Morag when her sister arrived. I am looking forward to you meeting my husband Tony. He is a lovely man. Imagine you having a baby, Bridget, aren't you lucky! We are trying for one; we would both like a big family.'

Just exactly as Elizabeth had said, they did arrive on the doorstep a few days later. It was wonderful seeing her again and she was right about her husband—he was nice and he just doted on her.

It was so strange, Bridget thought. A few months ago she was alone in the world and now here she was, surrounded by family. That night all the cousins arrived and the talking went on into the early morning. At one point Mo informed them that a friend was coming to stay with them. Mack the Fiddle, he was called, and they all laughed at the name.

"Why?" Elizabeth asked. "Is he a crook?"

Mo laughed so heartily that they thought she would choke.

"No, he's called that because he plays the fiddle! In fact, he is the best fiddler in the whole of Ireland. Now, what do I do to book the village hall? We will have a dance to welcome you and your husband, Elizabeth."

"That's my Mo," Shamus said, "any excuse for a dance."

"But I can't go," Bridget said. "There will be no one to look after the baby."

"But you will be taking the baby with you. In Ireland the whole family turns out, babies, grannies, granddads, the lot! And we all have a great time. New we had better get cracking; we will need to find out if the hall is free on Saturday night and we will put posters out all over Fada and, of course, we will have to have tea and things to eat." She dug Shamus in the ribs.

"We will show them how to dance an Irish Jig!" Shamus flung out his hands "Well, folks, when Mo gets an idea in her head, there's no stopping her, so you might as well just go along with her."

By the Saturday everything was organised. It seemed as if the whole island was going to the dance. Long tables were laid out at one side of the hall and women were soon bringing baking and sandwiches. Mo had the whole island running around.

"She is just wonderful!" Bridget said to Elizabeth.

"What a lady," Tony agreed.

The dance was a huge success. Mo was right, baby Jack slept through all the noise and the old grannies and granddads enjoyed the dance as much as the young ones and Mo and Shamus did lead the floor dancing an Irish Jig. Bridget, Elizabeth, the baby and Tony all decided to walk home. It was a beautiful moonlit night. Tony put his arm round Elizabeth and Bridget heard him whisper:

"I am so glad I married you, Elizabeth Ryan."

Something clutched at her heart she suddenly felt s lonely. Would anyone ever say something like that to her?

When she was lying in bed she made up her mind. "I must go to see Fada House." Elizabeth had spoken about it earlier.

"I'll come with you, Bridget. I would love to see it again."

Bridget didn't want that—she wanted to go on her own. She couldn't explain it. After the dance everything settled down. The Irish family were kept busy getting their stables ready and Bridget walked miles with the go-chair, renewing her acquaintance with all the corners of the island she had explored as a child. At one point she was very close to Fada House, but she turned back, telling herself it was too late in the day. Maybe she would go and spend the whole day there with the baby.

Elizabeth and Tony were away most of the time as they only had a few weeks in Scotland and they wanted to see as much of it as possible before going back to America. Elizabeth was calling America home now and Bridget was glad for her, for she seemed so happy. One morning, when they were cooking breakfast, Elizabeth turned to her.

"Do you ever see John MacInnes when you are about the island?"

Bridget felt her face go scarlet at the mention of his name.

Elizabeth laughed. "Do you remember the huge crush you had on him when we were kids and, by golly, didn't he have a crush on you! From what I hear he has done very well for himself."

Bridget just ignored her. Why was everyone talking about John MacInnes? After all, when they were teenagers they were told to keep away from him because he would turn out like his father. Well, they were all proved wrong; his poor father had loved John and his mother and as she was walking along the cliff road one day she was careful, remembering what had happened to John's father. It was now well fenced off and she came across a beautiful headstone erected, with love, to a good husband and father. She knelt down and said a prayer. She gathered some wild flowers and placed them by the stone. How sad life can be.

When she got home her young brother was sitting by the fire.

"I put some more peat on. I hope you don't mind."

"Of course I don't mind. It's so lovely to see you. Wait till I put the kettle on and we can have a long talk."

"That's why I'm here, Bridget. I want you to tell me everything since you were a little girl in Loadie."

*   *   *   *

She came in sight of the house and stood still. If anything, it was more beautiful than she remembered.

Then she remembered it seemed to glow when the early morning sun shone through the mist. She made her way to the garden. There were still some late roses in bloom and the sweet smell of honeysuckle filled the air. She sat on a seat and looked around. The garden was just as she remembered but she was amazed again when she noticed how well kept the garden was.

"What are you doing here, Bridget Ryan?"

The voice made her jump. It was Bogie Roll, as usual creeping about.

"I have always had permission to be here," Bridget said.

"But that was from the old owners. There is a new owner now so be off with you."

A man's voice spoke: "Now, I'm sure the new owners wouldn't mind Bridget being here."

Bridget looked up. John MacInnes was standing at her side. "I heard you were back, Bridget. That's a fine wee boy you have there."

Bridget's face burned scarlet. She put her hand up to hide it. How many times had she thought about the man standing before her! He put out his hand and, dreamlike, she held it.

"Would you like to come up to the house and have a look around? I am sure Bogie wouldn't mind?"

Bogie scowled and slinked away.

Bridget, still in a dream, made her way with John to the house. John reached into the go-chair and lifted the baby. The house was exactly as she remembered.

"Its so beautiful," she breathed.

She noticed that there was a newness about some of the curtains and carpets, though the colours were as she remembered them.

"A lot of things were pretty done, but they were replaced with as near the old ones as possible."

Bridget looked at John. "How did you know that?"

He smiled. "Haven't you guessed yet, Bridget? Fada House is mine."

Bridget stared at him, her mouth wide with surprise. He reached out and gently placed his hand over it.

"You will catch flies Bridget Ryan," he said, laughing at her. "I had a dream, Bridget, that one day I would own a beautiful house and when the estate was sold I persuaded William to sell Fada House to me. I am a wealthy man now, Bridget, but the other part of my dream was that you would share it with me. I knew you loved this house—that is why I have tried to keep it exactly as it was. I have always loved you, Bridget, from the first day you came to school."

"I think I must have loved you, John MacInnes, from that first day as well when you were showing off your new tackily boots. But I have made such a mess of my life, John. I love my baby but I feel nothing but contempt for his father. I was a stupid girl, taken in by him. I don't expect you to take on another man's child."

"Oh, Bridget, don't think like that! He is your child and because he is part of you I will love him."

Bridget breathed: "I feel I'm living in a fairy tale."

He held her lightly in his arms. "Will you marry me, Bridget?"

The baby gurgled and smiled up at him.

"Look, he approves, you must say yes!"

"Yes, yes, yes, John MacInnes!"

There was a cough from the door. Bogie Roll was actually smiling at them.

CHAPTER 13

▼

Bridget, sitting in the Rose Garden on this late September day, thought to herself how the garden and house had never lost it's magic for her throughout all the years. The sun was warm on her face, the perfume of the roses heady and strong. It was as if they were giving out their last burst of glory before the cold frosts that lurked round the corner came to destroy them.

Bridget closed her eyes, and with the gentle buzzing of the bees among the roses, she let her mind drift backwards and forwards over the years.

She remembered the first time she had set eyes on this garden and beautiful Fada House. It was like a house from a fairy tale. She still had to pinch herself to believe that it was now her home. She remembered the look of joy on John's face when she told him she would marry him.

She had been sitting in the garden when John had arrived back from one of his frequent business trips to Glasgow. His arms seemed to be full of boxes all beautifully wrapped in silver and gold. She found out later that the colours were used by one of the most expensive stores in Glasgow, and throughout the years she was to receive many more gifts with this wrapping.

She hugged herself, because even now after so many years she still remembered the thrill when she opened the largest box. Nestling in layers of tissue paper had been the most beautiful dress she had ever seen—yards and yards of the softest cream velvet, falling from a neckline of cream lace. In the smaller box were cream satin shoes. Even today she felt the tears come to her eyes when she remembered looking at herself in the mirror, the dress a perfect fit. John had been waiting downstairs; he had looked so disappointed, like a small boy.

"You don't like the dress? Why aren't you letting me see it on you?" Dear John, so kind and so sensitive.

"Don't you know, John?" she remembered saying. "You must not see the bride in her dress before the wedding."

And what a wedding it had been! It seemed as if the whole of Fada was celebrating with them, with dances and celidhs. She remembered the gasps from the congregation when she had walked down the aisle on William's arm. William had offered to take the part of her father and give her away. There were whispers of "she looks so beautiful, just like a princess"—and she felt like one.

She remembered John's delight when baby Elizabeth was born. "Oh Bridget, you have made me the happiest man in the world!"

Bridget's memories flooded back, of all the wonderfully happy days with John and the children, all her Irish family round her—they always seemed to be full of laughter. Dear William was always there, strong and steadfast. He loved Fada—it must have broken his heart when he had to sell it, but he was glad that it was people he loved that had bought it.

Again Bridget's mind leapt forward. She hugged herself. She felt a chill—when did things change?

Everything had been so wonderful. John's business was doing well, his boats sailing with cargo between Ireland and Glasgow. When Bridget visited the offices they were a hive of activity. She wanted to be there to help but John would not here of it. "My wife does not work—you have enough to do looking after the children."

William on his frequent visits to Fada taught her all the history of the island. They rode for miles, stopping at some of the croft cottages to collect all the produce. They were such happy days and the sun always seemed to be shining.

There was happiness and contentment all around.

When did it all change? She couldn't quit remember—she had been so wrapped up in her own life.

She seldom read newspapers. John had talked about a lot of unrest in Europe. She wasn't really interested—what did it matter what was going on there? This was Fada, a separate world. How wrong she had been.

She had been busy in the dining room. About twenty guests were coming. She loved this room; the large dark oak table gleamed with years of polishing and all the silver that William had begged them to use. "What use is it to me?" he had said. "It's rightful place is here at Fada House."

She remembered, then, getting a strange feeling. What if William did get married? He was a handsome man and she knew of lots of girlfriends he had had who would have leapt at the chance of marrying him. And if he did marry, the deep friendship between them would never be the same.

She had been so lost in her own thoughts she hadn't noticed John coming into the room. He stood white-faced looking at her.

"Bridget." He held her tightly. "We are at war. Britain is at war with Germany." She still couldn't understand. John tried to explain to her. In a small country that neither of them had heard of called Serbia, apparently a Serb had killed the heir to the Austrian Empire. The Austrians threatened to go to war with Serbia and Germany had joined forces with them.

Bridget still did not understand. "I find it difficult, myself," John had admitted. "The German armies marched through Belgium. The King of Belgium couldn't stop them. He asked for British help, which had been promised to them. So here we are at war." He shook his head. "You know Bridget, nothing will ever be the same again."

John had been right—nothing was ever the same. And one day William appeared wearing a soldier's uniform.

"I felt that I had to enlist," he had explained. "Lots of my friends have joined up. Nobody expects the war to last more than a few months."

So it had begun. Even on Fada the war was felt. Nearly all the young men had enlisted.

John had been restless. Terrible reports had been coming through of the suffering of the boys on the front line. And boys they had been, some as young as fifteen, lying about their age just to get into what they believed 'the glory of war'.

Most of John's boats had been taken over by the Navy. Germany was sinking merchant ships carrying food to Britain in the hope that Britain would surrender through starvation.

When John had arrived home one day and told her he had enlisted, it came as no shock. She had been expecting it.

Bridget turned and twisted on the garden seat, hugging herself to shut out the sad memory of saying goodbye to John.

"I don't want you to come to the pier, Bridget. I want to think of you at Fada House." Oh, the loneliness she had felt when he had gone!

She had kept busy. Most of the garden had been turned into growing vegetables and part of the House turned into a convalescent home for the servicemen returning from the Front, the peace of the island helping shattered nerves.

Many weeks had passed before John's letter had arrived. He was on a ship somewhere in the Atlantic on a convoy guarding merchant ships.

Four years into that awful war William had arrived at Fada House. By some quirk of fate he had been sent there to convalesce after weeks of surgery on a leg damaged by shrapnel.

William had been with her on that awful day. She had been busy, she remembered, weeding the vegetable garden. William had sat watching, unable to help and moaning about being unable to help.

They had both looked up as the postman approached them. He walked slowly up to them. She clutched her chest, remembering the postman had handed her the telegram. "I am so, so sorry, Mrs MacInnes," he had said.

William had steadied her as she read.

John, her dear beloved husband, was lost at sea.

How can one's body survive such a shock? She had little recollection of the weeks that followed.

Later she had learned that John's ship had been blown up. There had been no survivors.

Life did go on. The children had helped. She had to pull herself together for them. The terrible years of war had passed but something had gone from the island. Very few families had escaped unscathed.

Bridget sighed, half asleep. Where had all the years gone. So many people had passed through her life.

She smiled to herself. Bogie Roll had gone now for many years, though some of the roses he had tended so faithfully were still there.

John's kind mother who had helped her so much in her early years on Fada had died. She had been spared the war and the death of her only son.

Jack's father had been killed, not in the war but in a car accident in Aberdeen Through the years she had heard nothing about him. He was not a bad man. His whole life had been dominated by his possessive mother. Jack had been told by her at an early age about his father. She remembered him saying, "John is my dad, I love him and I know he loves me."

The Irish cousins had arrived one day at Fada House. Her dear young brother, looking so much older than his young years, had hugged her. "Bridget, we're all going back to Ireland. I am going to miss you but we will always stay close. I can't settle since the war. I might even go to visit sister Elizabeth in America."

Bridget had never felt so lonely, even though she had kept busy getting the house and garden back to normal.

And so the years went. Jack and Elizabeth both at university. Elizabeth at Glasgow, studying law, and Jack at Edinburgh since an early age wanting to be a doctor.

She had walked down to Maggie's old cottage one afternoon. It was more or less a ruin now. Fishermen were using it as a bothy. She had sat there by the cold empty range and the tears had come.

She had felt a hand on her shoulder.

"Dear, dear Bridget, why all the tears?" William had appeared so quietly. "Come now back to the house. We will have tea, then I want to show you something I have bought you."

She remembered laying her head on his chest and felt such a feeling of contentment. "How could I ever do without you, William?" she remembered saying.

And it seemed the most natural thing in the world when he said, "You don't have to be without me, Bridget. I have always loved you. I know that I can never replace John but I want to marry you."

"I love you too, William, in a different way from the love I had for John. I am never happier than when you are near me."

They had wandered happily back to Fada House, talking about the day they would marry.

"Come now, Bridget," William had said. "Come and see your present."

They wandered down the garden to a nearby field. Two horses were grazing peacefully.

"Yours and mine," William smiled. "It will be like the old days, riding round the island."

Bridget remembered throwing her arms around his neck and kissing him. "I am so lucky, William, to have your love."

Someone was shaking her. "Wake up, Bridget. The sun has gone and you are getting cold."

Bridget woke, lifting her head sleepily.

"Oh William, it's you. Help me up. I seem to have lost my stick."

They wandered back to the house, both white haired—both in the autumn of their years but both still very much in love.

THE END

978-0-595-47199-7
0-595-47199-4

Printed in the United Kingdom
by Lightning Source UK Ltd.
124852UK00001B/286-384/A